Secrets Never Stay Buried

Dolly Howard

Contents

Prologue

It was a cold spring morning in the city, and Kim wanted to do was go back to bed. She had been up since six that morning, like every other and was coming home from her dance practice a couple of blocks away from her apartment.

Everywhere was icy, the ground was covered with a sprinkle of snow and she was freezing. She snuggled closer into her jacket as she waited at the side of the road for the traffic to pass. Kim was in some sort of a daze that she hadn't even noticed the car stopped beside her and the green light for her to walk. There were few people out at this hour and so only one car waited for her to cross the road.

The loud beep of a car horn broke through her day dream and startled her. Kim jumped involuntarily out of her spot and slipped on the icy footpath beneath her. She fell to the ground with a thud and angrily groaned at the idiotic driver for ever beeping in the first place.

The driver quickly jumped out of his car when he saw she hadn't moved from the ground. She was lying facing upwards to the sky above her, already feeling some pain in her back. Kim had just done a half hour of cardio and an hour of dance practice- she really just wanted to be left there on the cold ground to bask in complete embarrassment of herself.

"Are you okay?" she heard a male voice ask as it got closer to her. She opened her eyes to meet a crystal blue pair blinking down at her- concern laced in his expression.

"Do I fucking look alright? Why the hell did you honk at me?" despite his clear good looks, Kim was not in any mood to flirt with this gorgeous man standing over her.

"I'm so sorry Ms. You weren't moving, I just wanted to let you know you could cross." His voice was apologetic and sweet- maybe a little too sweet, she thought.

"Well that worked out great didn't it." She spat sarcastically. Kim saw him kneel beside her then, he began to help her up but she stopped him.

"Let me help you up-"

"No, it's fine. I can get up myself." Kim didn't want to feel any more embarrassed in front of this beautiful stranger.

Although she was struggling to get up and continued to slip and slide on the ice, she kept going. He stifled a laugh at the sight of her.

"Are you laughing at me?" Kim squinted her eyes, her annoyance beginning to wear off by then.

"Maybe a little." He chuckled and she gave up, falling on the ground again. Kim let out a loud laugh at herself- this would only happen to her, she thought. "Just let me help you." The man said gently. She allowed him to do so this time and in seconds, she was standing up again. He held her arm while she steadied herself.

"Thank you, I'm fine now." Kim couldn't help but blush once she got a closer look at him. His hair was a chocolate brown, his jaw clenched as he continued to hold onto her arm and his pink lips were pursed together in order to stop another laugh from escaping them.

"Are you sure that when I let you go you won't fall again?" he looked into her eyes with his bright blue ones. He was cute, she thought, and his smile was contagious. He left her without a word to say, all she could do was nod slowly.

The man loosened his grip on her arm and she stood on her own then.

"Thank you." She said a little shyly.

"I'm really sorry, it was my fault." His voice trailed off.

There was a silence for a moment, the two done nothing but look at each other. Not a word was said by either. His eyes lingered on her lips and she noticed this so moved her head an inch or two away from his.

"I better get going."

Kim had to stop herself from rolling her eyes at the scene that had just unfolded before her. How cliché, how perfect he seemed to be- looks and demeanor- It was all too good to be true. The fact that she would happen to meet a faultless man on the street and feel something the second she looked into his eyes. What a load of bullshit, she thought. Things were never that straight forward for her, especially in the boyfriend department.

She gave him a polite smile, before turning to walk away but he grabbed her hand to stop her. She turned around and saw his hopeful eyes.

"I'd like to make it up to you..." The stranger gave her a small, shy smile and she had to hold in a snort. Shy? This man? She didn't think so. He had this aura of confidence coming off of him. Despite not having any reason to doubt he was being genuine, Kim doubted it regardless. Men were assholes, at least that was what she thought anyway. She had learned that the hard way and would never change her mind on that. Ever.

"How?" she continued on with this ridiculous conversation despite everything she thought.

"Maybe dinner? Or coffee?"

"I'm sorry, that would be great but I'm not really looking for anything like that at the moment. Thanks anyway, I have to go now." Kim rejected him but regretted it once she saw the wounded look on his face. He let her go and she began on her way again, back to her apartment.

She wondered why she had felt bad about saying no, it wasn't like she knew him? Maybe Kim was being too much of a pessimist, not everyone was the same. It was an unfair conclusion to come to about men but she couldn't help herself. She was sick of all of the men in her life being nothing but disappointments- her father being one of them.

Kim let out a long sigh once she closed the door of her apartment and set her keys down on her counter. She showered, threw on a pair of baggy sweatpants and a sport bra before making her way into her bedroom for a nap. She felt wore out and her muscles ached from her training earlier. She drifted off thinking about the man she had met earlier, thinking she wouldn't see him again but she was wrong.

She would meet him again sooner than she thought.

Chapter 1

Kim lived alone. Ever since she moved to Portland, she had always preferred to have her own space although her friends there had asked a number of times to share a place somewhere. So the fact that she woke up to the sound of a man's voice outside her bedroom, startled her.

She had closed her curtains her bedroom but the light from the afternoon day outside was streaming into the room through the thin drapes. Kim thought she may have been dreaming, so turned over in bed under the covers, mumbling something to herself.

"Yes I have her right here sir... No, not yet... She's asleep."

That was the point in the conversation when Kim's eyes shot open and she jumped up out of bed, her eyes wide with surprise. Kim noticed how her drawers in her room and wardrobe had been pulled apart, as if someone was looking for something. She still doubted herself and thought she was dreaming but there was no time to think about that by then. The man had stopped speaking and turned to face her, looking at her through the open door.

Kim looked in astonishment at the man she had seen earlier that morning. When he had helped her up, his voice was kind and his expression warm- but he was different this time. His features were hard, his eyes cold and his voice was just above a growl.

"I'll have to call you back sir." He said after a short silence between the pair.

Kim knew that being stood frozen in her spot was not going to help her in this situation. And also that he would not be standing a great distance away from her for long. The kind man from earlier had disappeared and had been replaced with this dangerous looking one. She knew the outcome of this could not be good. She needed to think but she had a mind block.

The stranger was the first to move; it took him one step before she ran at her door and managed to slam it shut.

"Open the fucking door." He said as he smashed his fist onto the wood and tried to force his way through.

Kim continued to hold it shut but knew it wouldn't be long before he kicked his way into the room. She struggled and then all at once, quickly let go of the door. It swung open and he stumbled through. As he got his bearings, Kim ran through the open doorway and down her hall into her kitchen but he was hot on her tail. She stood behind the island and gripped the countertop with her hands tightly as she looked at him. He was on the opposite side and seemed to be a lot calmer than she was.

"Get the fuck out of my apartment you creep!" Kim exclaimed, trying to catch her breath and stop herself from hyperventilating.

She saw how a wicked grin crossed his face and his eyes darkened. She gulped when she noticed his calm and cool exterior. They ran in a circle around the island and she landed back where she had begun.

"And if I don't? What are you going to do about it sweetheart?" he raised a dark brow at her.

"I'll- I... I'll call the cops."

"You're going to call the cops?" he snorted. "You won't get very far by calling the cops sweetheart."

"Stop calling me that." She cringed and quickly opened the top drawer in front of her that was filled with cutlery but nothing sharp enough to use as a weapon.

The man had made his way to the side of the island and his huge body was in full view to her. Kim looked from the knives and forks towards the man a couple of times as he inched his way towards her. Quickly without much though, she picked up a butter knife and held it up in an attempt to fight him off. He burst into laughter at the sight of this stupid girl.

"Is that the best you've got? A fucking butter knife? You're going to have to do much better than that to scare me off. What are you going to do? Stab me? That thing's not even sharp..." He made a good point.

"No, but they are quite heavy if you ask me."

She weighed it in her hand before throwing it quickly at his face. It hit him between the eyes, causing him to scrunch up his eyebrows in agitation. Kim threw another knife, this time it hit him in the eye, then she threw another and another. He thought it was more annoying than painful. Then she picked up her last knife and aimed carefully. It hit him just below the waist, between the legs just as she had hoped for.

"Ah! You fucking bitch." He grunted out as she ran for dear life. But she didn't get very far before he caught up with her.

Kim was only metres away from her front door before he pinned her to the wall, his body pressed up against her with great force.

"Get off of me!" she squealed, feeling his body so close. He put his hand across her mouth to stop her from making any noise.

"Care to take me up on that offer of dinner again sweetheart?" His face was but a breath away from hers. She stopped squirming for a moment or two as their eyes met. Kim's gaze was fixated on this beautiful man that stood in front of her. "I'll make it worth your while." He grinded against her for a second, pressing her further into the wall before letting out an evil laugh. Kim's brows furrowed and she bit his hand. Once he took it away she opened her mouth to speak.

"I knew it was too good to be true! Why do all men turn out to be assholes in the end?" Kim exclaimed angrily but he only laughed again at her.

She tried her best to push him off of her but he wouldn't budge. It was then she decided to use every last bit of energy she had in her to reach up and slap him across the face. He was more shocked than hurt. His grip loosened on her and she managed to get free of him, only for him to lunge at her again.

"I've had enough of this. I thought I might get your hopes up a little and allow you to think you're going to get away but you and I both know that's never going to happen."

"What do you want from me?" Kim asked, terrified of what this physco might do to her.

She remembered the fact that her neighbours on either side had nine to five, normal jobs and were probably at work at that time. Even if they weren't they wouldn't call for help if she screamed her apartment down. They had gotten into countless fights with Kim over the past couple of months of occupying the complex about how she always played her music too high and the fact that she kept inviting one neighbour's cat into her apartment without permission.

"Oh you'll find out soon, don't worry." He had her pinned to the floor, his heavy body on top of hers. All the while Kim couldn't help but think that only an hour or two ago she would've loved to have him like this. But now she was glad she had declined this pig's offer of a date- she knew better. "You're not leaving this apartment until I drag you out of it with me sweetheart. Now sit still."

Kim continued to struggle beneath him, despite his threats. He forced her flat against the ground, keeping her put with one hand on her chest as the other searched in his pocket for something. Kim scratched at his face and clawed at his dark suit, in a failed attempt to keep him this short distance away from her despite knowing she would not be able to get out of this situation. She had no more options left but to lie there and wait for whatever would happen, happen.

He poured an unknown substance onto a white cloth. Kim's eyes widened with complete terror at the sight of his actions. A million questions raced through her head at once while she was trying to figure out what there was left to do. The man was strong and seemed willing to do anything he needed to get hold of her.

"What do you want from me?" she screamed out, surprised he hadn't yet covered her mouth.

He looked down at her with reluctance etched onto his face. He was hesitating and she wondered why. His holding back had made her become completely still under him- it gave her a small glimmer of hope that he might let her go. But soon enough, he stopped staring at her and answered.

"I don't want anything from you, but someone else does..." a ghost of a menacing smile fell upon his lips before he placed the cloth forcefully over her mouth and nose.

Kim struggled against his, gripping onto his crisp dress shirt and clawing at him but it was no use. There was only a certain amount of time she could spend holding her breath before she eventually breathed in the chemicals he had given her. In a matter of seconds, her eyes began to roll into the back of her head and they fell shut. Her last thought being:

What would happen when she woke up?

Chapter 2

Kim woke to the sound of air conditioning in an unknown car. To say she felt terrible was an understatement. She groaned groggily, blinking the sleep from her eyes. Her head felt heavy but light at the same time. Kim let out a sigh in pain again as she closed her eyes, not yet ready to take in her surroundings.

"You keep moaning like that sweetheart and I'll have to pull over and give you a reason to moan."

His voice was velvety and menacing, Kim would go as far enough to even describe it as sexy, if he wasn't a physco who had kidnapped her that is... It caused her eyes to shoot open and look to her side, to find him driving. Kim looked around in a state of panic at the bright dirt roads ahead of them, there was not another car or hint of civilisation to be seen for miles. She squirmed and tried to move but felt the cold metal of handcuffs around her wrists.

"You're a pig! Get me out of these damn things now so I can beat your ass." She threatened but only got a bout of condescending laughter in return.

"Stop trying to get free, I have the key and you won't be un-cuffed until I say so."

After a moment or two of trying to escape the handcuffs and also trying to unlock the car door as it sped down the road,to find he had locked it, Kim had finally given up. The car fell silent and she decided she would behave for now in order to get answers out of this stranger.

"Why am I here?"

"Because you have something needed by someone else."

"And what would that be?"

"I think you know what I'm talking about Kim..." He turned for a second to look her in the eye. Kim had a faint idea of what he could have been looking for back at her apartment but did not allow him to know this. She refrained from showing anything on her face. She asked another question instead.

"Who is this someone else?"

"Never mind."

"Never mind? You have me handcuffed in a car alone with only you for company for however long we will be driving for and you won't even have a conversation with me? Who are you working for? What do you want from me because I don't know what you're talking about-"

"Give it a rest Kim."

"How do you know my name?"

"Because I know a lot about you, I've done my research."

"Ew, you creep. I bet you're a stalker. And if so, I swear to god as soon as you let me out of these things I'm going to make you regret all of this."

"It's my job." He snapped angrily at her and rolled his eyes.

"Whatever."

"Shut up."

"No."

"Yes."

"No! Why don't you just give me some answers here? I'm sure we have plenty of time to waste. Where are we going? Who do you work for? What's going to happen when we get out of this car? Are you a serial killer? Because you look like one." He gritted his teeth at the annoyance this girl was causing him.

"Just shut the hell up already!" he snapped for a second time, making Kim realise that he was a man with a temper. It was a pity she just did not care in the slightest. She had nothing much to live for at this point, her life had become boring and she needed some type of excitement- if she would be killed in the end of all of this, she wanted to at least be thrilled a little bit. "I was told to bring you back to my boss dead or alive, it really doesn't matter so for your own sake- I think you should just do what I say if you want to live." He lied, he knew he needed to keep her alive for his boss. They needed the location of the things she had stolen and information from her, there something else he wasn't told about yet but what did he care? He just wanted to get the job done, no matter what it took.

He was surprised that she had actually scoffed at his words and rolled her eyes. She was already driving him insane and she was awake no more than two minutes? How was he going to stand her for a whole road trip across the country? She lacked respect or sense of who was in charge here, practically laughing at his threat of killing her. He needed to think of a way to scare her then because of it.

Nathan Smith was not the type of man to be reckoned with, or laughed at for that matter either. He was always in control and would remain in control for however long it took him to bring this girl back to Washington D.C where his boss would handle her.

"I'm shaking." She said sarcastically, wanting to get a rise out of him soon.

Why not? She thought. Kim ignored every fibre within herself telling her this man was deadly, dangerous and also that he could probably kill her in a heartbeat. She was curious as to what way exactly he was going to explode in front of her. Her eyes trailed down to his huge hands that gripped onto the steering wheel in silent rage. His knuckles were beginning to turn white and she grinned.

"You know what? We'll see how long you'll be laughing when I pull this car over and throw you in the trunk." He warned her, to which she quietened down some.

Her expression dropped and she seemed a little taken aback. Nathan laughed wickedly and continued on driving, happy to have some quiet in the car again- but that would not last for very long.

"You know the biggest mistake you've made so far was not tying up my feet." He furrowed his brows at her words.

"W-" before he could even speak, Kim swung her legs up and kicked him in the face. She pressed her foot down on the steering wheel and maneuvered it so it turned very rapidly towards the side of the road.

He shouted in shock and quickly took hold of the steering wheel again, trying to stop the swerving car from going off track completely. Nathan turned the car quickly but Kim continued to try again.

"You little bitch." He grabbed her leg and twisted it until he saw pain on her face, his other hand still taking hold of the wheel.

"Ah!" she screamed out in agony and yanked her foot away swiftly.

Within a matter of seconds, Nathan had harshly pulled the car over and turned to pounce on her. He pinned her down with his heavy body and stared into her eyes with his crazy, wide, crystal blue ones. His breath fanned her cheek and she blinked, trying to calm the adrenaline coursing through her veins. Nathan had scrunched up her clothing roughly with his hands and held it close to his chest so she was mere centimetres away from his face.

She was a nuisance already and he wanted nothing to do with her, he thought in complete annoyance.

"What. The. Fuck. Was that?" he spit his words out.

Kim noticed how his face was a bright shade of raging red and it made her want to shrink back into her seat had he not been holding her by her shirt. She blinked a couple of times, her eyes wide with fright but he did not care. Nathan wanted her to be afraid of him, like everyone else was.

"Answer me!" he pushed her back roughly against the seat.

"Fuck you! I'm not answering any of your god damn questions until you answer some of mine!" she shouted back at him, crossing her arms one over the other.

"You're a sassy little one aren't you?" he breathed in and out deeply through his flared nostrils in an attempt to calm himself down and gain composure again.

"And you're an asshole!"

Nathan did not reply to Kim's comment for a moment. A wicked smile grew on his lips as he looked at her face. He leaned closer to her, their chests touching. Kim was frozen in her seat, wondering what was going to happen next when he brought his lips close to her ear. She took in the smell of his cologne and tried her best not to be affected by his close proximity.

"That's the nicest compliment I've ever gotten sweetheart." His lips grazed her ear as he whispered, his tone sultry and dark.

Kim's breath hitched in her throat at his words. He snatched something from the back seat behind her, what he had been leaning forward to get all along. She only realised it was cable tie by the time he moved to his own seat and grabbed both her ankles together in a vice grip. She tried to kick him again in order to free her legs but it was no use. In a matter of seconds, the cable tie was tightly restraining her legs from moving anywhere.

Before she knew it, he had yanked her out of the car and threw her over his shoulder, placing one hand on the back of her knees and the other on her behind to steady her as he walked with her. Kim turned her head to try and look at his face but it was impossible. All she got was the back of his head.

"Put me down you fool!" she tried to wriggle her way out of his arms. "And get your hand off my ass." He listened to neither of her requests and she soon realised where this was going. Nathan opened the trunk.

"No! No please..."she begged as he placed her in the dark trunk. "Please, I'm begging you to let me out. I promise I'll be good. I won't pull another stunt again, please." She was desperate but he only smiled at her foolishness. If he was to let her out now, she would never take him seriously. He needed to teach her a lesson and so he slammed the trunk closed before getting back into the car and driving off.

Chapter 3

"Time to get out Kim." Nathan smiled wickedly at the sight of her.

She had been curled up in a ball in his trunk, her eyes were not yet ready to adjust from the darkness to the daylight again. It was getting cloudy and the sun was already setting. She squinted at him and then rolled over. How long have I been in here? She wondered. Although it had felt like days, it was only a couple of hours.

Nathan parked in a half-deserted restaurant and decided to let her out for a bit of air. He wanted to get back to his boss as soon as possible but that meant driving for almost a week to get there. And with only Kim to keep him company, he knew he might lose his mind before the week was up.

Nathan hadn't even reached the border of Oregon yet and the girl he was keeping in his trunk was playing on his mind from the very beginning when she fell on the ice early that morning. But it was past eight then and he needed to eat and find somewhere to rest.

"No." Kim replied, her tone monotonous.

"We're getting something to eat."

"I'm not going anywhere with you, you physco."

"Get the hell out of the car now Kim." Nathan didn't seem phased by her words in any way.

"I said no." she gritted her teeth.

"I'll untie you?" his said persuasively. There was a long pause until she moved around in the trunk, trying to get herself out.

"I need help."

"Whatever." He scoffed but helped her out of the trunk anyway before pulling a knife out of nowhere and cutting her legs free. Kim stood up straight and looked into his eyes as he unlocked her handcuffs. Nathan's eyes never left hers, not even to look at what he was doing.

Kim grinned at him once she was free, it confused him but he allowed a small smile to creep up onto his lips. Just as he done so, he immediately regretted it. It took a moment for him to register what happened once Kim's hand came into contact with his face. Her slap was harsh and stung his cheek.

"That's for breaking into my apartment." Her voice was filled with rage. Then she used the back of her hand to slap his other cheek.

"That's for tying me up." She reached out to hit him again.

"And this is for-"

Nathan grabbed her wrist and crushed it between his fingers violently but with little force needed on her fragile hands.

"Not so fast Kim."

"Let me go! You're hurting me."

"You slap like a bitch." Nathan seemed so unaffected by her words or her hits, it made her frustration grow even more.

"That's because I am a bitch." She managed to yank her hand away and crossed her arms then. Her brows were furrowed and she was as angry as she could get right then. Nathan rolled his eyes at her statement and grabbed her waist, bringing her body to his side. He slammed the trunk closed and walked with her inside the building.

Although she squirmed and tried to get free of him, it was no use. Nathan bent down and whispered in her ear. His tone was stiff and left no room for argument. It scared and excited her at the same time. This man was going to be a problem. Considering he had kidnapped her and threw her in the trunk of his car- the fact that she had to stop herself from giving in to this pull he had on her was a little scary to her. What the hell was going on with her? She was more affected by him than any other man she had come across- he had to be the worst of them- and she had only met him this morning?

"If you even attempt to pull some sort of stunt in here... I promise you will regret it." His lips brushed roughly against her ear and made her shiver.

Nathan pulled away and waited for a member of staff to give them a table. Kim quietly followed by his side. It sur-prised him that she had yet to say anything. A perky blonde girl in her late teens greeted them with a wide smile and an keen tone. Kim knew she was smiling more so at the man beside her than the woman he had with him. She rolled her eyes at the young girl's eagerness.

Once seated, Nathan scanned through the menu, blatantly ignoring the waitresses' flirty smiles and laughter. Kim sat there, an irritated expression on her face, and stared at him.

"Aren't you going to get something to eat? My treat?" he taunted her as he looked up from his menu.

"I think I already declined that offer, don't you remember?" Kim wittily replied to which he let out a small condescending laugh.

"I remember you wanting to say yes but saying no..."

"I didn't want to say yes."

"You did, I could tell."

"Didn't."

"Did." The two bickered, Nathan needing to get the last word. Kim let out an aggravated breath and looked at him again.

"Even if I did want to say yes then, it wouldn't make a difference now, considering it was before I discovered you were a complete whacko."

"The names Nathan actually."

"Can I take your order?" the waitress was back again, cute and giggly as ever. It made Kim want to shake her head in disgust but she refrained from doing so.

She was surprised when Nathan ordered for not only himself, but her too.

"I thought I told you already – twice- that I didn't want to have dinner with you."

"Just have dinner with me, it would make me feel better for what I done earlier?" Nathan's sweet voice had come back and he batted his eyelashes at her. He turned into the man Kim saw that morning and it made her red with fury and slight embarrassment. He was mocking her for ever believing such a persona as the one he had become earlier.

"Whatever..." she rolled her eyes and he chuckled wickedly at her.

"You actually fell for it? God you're so stupid." She narrowed her eyes at his comment.

Her hand itched to picked up the glass of water next to her cutlery and throw it over his face. Nathan saw how her expression changed to one that held calculation and sorrow then. What was she thinking about? He wondered.

There was a tense silence at the table for a couple of minutes until their food arrived, food that Kim refused to eat.

"Dig in." he said monotonously, continuing to make a joke about all of this.

"You really are crazy aren't you? You're acting like this is normal, like you break into people's apartments and kidnap them on a daily basis. Do you? What the hell do you want from me anyway? Why are we here in this shitty restaurant and where are we going after this? You know, my friends will be looking for me pretty soon and they'll call the cops. Whatever you're up to, you're going to get caught."

"Funny how you said friends and not family." Nathan laughed bitterly at her. The fact that he had ignored every question she had asked made her even agrier.

"What has that got to do with anything?" Kim questioned, did he know? Did he know that she had no family left? And if so, why was he trying to make fun of her because of it?

"It's got everything to do with it little Kimmy."

"Don't call me that." she replied quickly. There was another silence as he began to eat his food but Kim couldn't take it anymore, she was about to explode with rage. "Well? Aren't you going to answer any of my damn questions? Do you want me to scream? Let everyone in this god damn restaurant know what you done to me today. I bet they'd call the cops and you'd have to answer to them instead of me-"

"You think the cops will get you out of this situation Kim?" his tone was disdainful and full of superiority. "I don't answer to anyone. You think the cops are going to help you? I'm above the cops; they can't do anything for you." His bitter laugh filled her ears and his words wrapped themselves around her lungs, leaving her breathless. Who would help her? What the hell was she going to do?

"What do you want from me?" Kim seemed to be asking all of the same questions. She was beyond confused as to what was happening around her.

"I told you already, I don't want something from you. It's someone else."

"Well what do they want from me?" she asked through gritted teeth.

"The files Kim. The information you stole from your father's company." He said with a straight face. The mention of her father left a bitter taste in her mouth. It was funny how just seconds ago she had wanted to talk until there was no air left in her lungs and now she had nothing else to say.

"You think I'd give them to you?" she was the one laughing bitterly at him then.

"You stole them, and we need them back."

"We? You work for my father?"

"No. The CIA."

"Well I'm afraid you're mistaken. I didn't steal anything from my father or his company."

"We have proof."

"You can't steal something that was already yours Nathan." She used his first name this time, trying to explain to him his mistake.

"What do you mean?"

"It doesn't matter." She shook her head, she wasn't ready to have this conversation with anyone. It was difficult for even herself to comprehend how it was that her father could steal her ideas and work from right under her nose. But come to think of it, it was her father after all. She could expect no less. "I destroyed them five years ago when I took them back. So if that's what you were looking for in my apartment, you won't ever find them. Why are they so important to you anyway? They were just business deals not yet made on a product I hadn't quite thought through yet. Nothing was set in stone, no deals were officially made, they should mean nothing at all to you."

"You expect me to believe you got rid of important and confidential files that you spent so much time and effort trying to steal?" he scoffed.

"I told you already they were mine to begin with!" she thumped her hand loudly on the table, causing the cutlery to clink and heads to turn.

Her nostrils flared and her cheeks burned with complete fury. She stood up quickly and made her way out of the restaurant quickly. Nathan was hot on her tail after placing a number of bills down on the table and grabbing his coat. She wasn't the only one furious then.

Kim had begun making her way out of the car park, close to passing his car that he had brought her here in. Nathan stormed towards her protruding back and caught her shoulder before she could make it any farther away. His scorching gaze burned her eyes and anywhere else his eyes caught sight of.

"I thought I told you not to cause a scene." His voice was low, it was filled with anger and resentment. It shook her up a little, that and the sight of him in all his rage.

Nathan pushed her against the side of his car before roughly grabbing her waist so she couldn't move anywhere. That was something that was not necessary. Kim was frightened to within an inch of her life, more so than when she found him rummaging around her apartment. She was afraid he would kill her right there and then. Her eyes were wide with shock, her legs like jelly as he held her close to him.

Nathan placed his fingers delicately under her chin and tilted it up so her gaze met his. She gulped and he laughed wickedly at the sight of her. Her breath hitched in her throat, she was unable to say a word. His chest was flush against hers and he reached out then to tuck a strand of hair behind her ear.

"Are you scared Kim?" he asked, somehow liking the terrified look in her eyes. He was a monster, a heartless one too. He knew that for sure. But that was why he was so good at his job. He worked alone and only alone. Those were his rules.

"Because you should be."

Chapter 4

"Because you should be."

They were so dangerously close to each other in that moment. Close enough for her to stupidly inhale his scent and warm to the feeling of his arm hooked around her waist. But she needed to snap out of it? This man was merely a stranger, a dangerous one at that. He could kill her in an instant and had already said he would if he felt like it.

"Say something sweetheart..." he whispered in her ear, turning her legs to jelly. She was more than a little surprised to feel his lips brush lightly against her jawline, placing soft kisses as he went. Wasn't he just majorly pissed a minute ago? She thought in confusion.

Kim had to stop herself from moaning at the close contact from Nathan. He lifted her shirt a little so his fingertips could feel her soft skin. Kim shivered in delight and he liked knowing she could be easily affected by him- it would help him in the future if ever he needed to use this trick of his.

She began to realise that she was more frightened than she had ever been before in her life and wonder what had gotten into her. Where had the fierce Kim gone? Where was the fearless Kim hiding? What had happened to the brave Kim? Was she allowing some man- dangerous or not- to control her actions? She had allowed her father to control her for too long, she would not let anyone but herself decide what she done ever again.

Kim found herself again and pushed Nathan abruptly away from her, just as he thought his plan was working. He looked at her in confusion once he saw a pair of furious eyes burning holes into his face. But as soon as his confusion had arrived on his face, it had departed- making him look unaffected again, even slightly bored.

"Get the hell off of me you creep!" she exclaimed and tried to cross her arms but then she felt Nathan swiftly take her wrists and snap something onto them.

"What the-"

"I told you already the names Nathan sweetheart, and I'd really prefer if you called me by that instead of creep or physco or whatever else you come up with. Now get in the car."

Nathan was unphased by her continuous whining and bickering at him. Although it was quite humorous to watch, Nathan was in no mood at that moment. He was tired and needed to find a place to stay for the night. They both had an early start the next morning and were in need of some sleep.

"No." she said out straight with some kind of pride behind it that confused Nathan. No wasn't an option for her, so it made him wonder why she had even thought about not doing as he said.

"Unless you want me to tie your legs up again and throw you in the trunk Kim... I suggest you get your skinny little ass into the goddamn car before this turns from zero to a hundred really quick. Maybe I'll give you more of those answers you're looking for eh?" he taunted her and spoke with finality.

Despite wanting to put up a fight, Kim felt exhausted from the new information she had gathered. Her thoughts were running wild. What did her father have to do with all of this? She knew that taking back what was hers all those years ago would come back to haunt her but not like this.

Kim remained silent in the car ride to wherever Nathan was taking her. She did not care. Her thoughts were too much to deal with at that time and she needed to reflect. There was no time to be pushing Nathan's buttons, wondering what could happen next. He sensed her quietness and flicked his eyes from the road to her a couple of times. She failed to notice this or acknowledge him, but sat there staring vacantly out the windscreen at the road ahead.

Nathan decided to say nothing too, but observed her face full of sorrow with curiosity. He wanted to know what was going on inside that head of hers but pushed that thought away to think about the issue at hand: a place to stay the night. After a couple of minutes driving through the small town, he managed to find a dingy motel and pulled in as soon as he spotted it.

Kim stayed in the car while he organised a room to stay in. She would have noticed him knocking on the car window next to her had she not been recollecting everything that led up to the day she decided to stand up for herself. She left everyone she had ever known without saying goodbye, not that she felt it was needed anyway- she didn't want to stay minute longer in Chicago.

Everyone there, her family, and friends, even her own fiancé had deceived her. She knew she deserved better so moved on to Portland to make something of herself there, without the influence of her well known family or her father's world renowned technology company.

"Kim!" Nathan's voice immediately snapped her out of her thoughts.

Her head shot to the side to find him peering in the window at her, his thick brows furrowed in annoyance. She shook her head, as if the simple task would rid her mind of the heavy thoughts and unbuckled her seatbelt as quickly as she could considering she was handcuffed.

"I'm sorry. I didn't hear you." Her voice was the sweetest he had ever heard it since he met her earlier that day. It was soft, gentle and sounded as if she was somewhere else.

Nathan could tell she was tired, her eyes were sleepy and she was calm, a little too calm for his liking. He could tell there was something bothering her, something other than any of the events that had happened previously that day.

Once he opened the door with his key, he threw his dark duffle bag on the double bed and looked around the room. Kim's thoughts had travelled back to the situation at hand, like what was going to happen next?

"You better go to bed. We need some sleep for our journey tomorrow." Nathan's voice returned to its dark and serious tone from earlier.

"Where are we going?" Kim tried to stop herself form fidgeting with her hands to avoid any eye contact.

Nathan sat on the bed and retrieved something to sleep in from the bag. He kicked off his shoes and slid his suit jacket off. She almost thought what she had asked would be another ignored question to add to the list from that day but eventually, he spoke.

"I'm taking you to D.C. where my boss will decide what to do with you."

"But I haven't done anything? Those files that I took back belonged to me. It's my father who should have been the one taken and hauled back to D.C. Not me."

"Look, it's orders from above. You're going to D.C. with me, whether I have to drag you there or not."

Nathan had researched a lot about Kim but didn't know as much as he let on to know about the situation and what she had stolen from her father. He didn't quite understand everything that was going on around him but went along with it anyway. He knew he had to trust whatever orders he was given. There was something the people above weren't telling him, something was missing from their explanation.

Although Kim may have thought Nathan was the enemy, she had the whole thing entirely wrong. Nathan was told to keep her safe, to make sure she was unharmed when they returned to D.C. The enemy though, was not too far behind them. Nathan hadn't been the only one looking for Kim out there. There were others too, ones that were more dangerous than he could ever be.

She didn't know it yet, but this situation was a lot more serious than she could ever anticipate. All Nathan knew was that those documents and files she stole from her father were very important ones. And what she had done pissed a lot of people off.

"Didn't you say you worked for the CIA?" She questioned, trying to understand all of this.

"Yes." He said before tossing her a familiar pyjama set. It was hard for her to catch considering she was still in hand-cuffs but she caught them anyway.

"Aren't they the ones who look after foreign affairs and threats? Not stuff regarding a US based technology company."

"Your father deals and associates with powerful people from around the globe. I thought you would have known that considering you worked for Scott Inc. for quite some time before moving away." Was all he said.

He watched carefully as she looked down at the pyjamas, waiting for her reaction. Kim's face reddened quickly and she slowly looked up from her pink, care bear pyjamas to meet Nathan's eyes. He had a smug smile on his face, it was almost too sexy for her to mad at him, note the word almost.

"Where did you get these?" Kim asked as he laughed at her embarrassment.

"Aren't you like twenty-five?" he sniggered at her.

"Twenty-six actually." Kim mumbled. She felt self-conscious under his stare then. She was getting defensive and he found that even more humorous.

"Why did you go through my things? It's none of your business what I wear to bed."

"I would have liked to think you wore nothing at all sweetheart." He wandered into the bathroom, leaving her to get dressed in a pair of handcuffs which was near impossible. He left the door slightly ajar and called out, "What a disappointment."

Kim rolled her eyes at his statement and managed to remove her sweatpants. She slid her care bear pyjama bottoms up her legs but was struggling to remove her top. Nathan came back into the room dressed in a dark tee and boxer shorts but she was unaware of his presence. He watched as she continued to lift her t-shirt over her head and stifled a snort.

"Why don't you fucking take these handcuffs off so I can maybe get into my care bear pyjamas you wanted me to wear so fucking much?" she almost shouted, thinking he was still in the bathroom.

She was clearly agitated and her voice broke a little, like she was about to cry but she swallowed back her tears. It took everything in her to do that but she done it without hesitation. Kim didn't want to look weak in front of him by breaking down. She didn't want to get dressed, she didn't want to go to bed, she definitely didn't want to go to D.C.

What she did want to do was to go home, back to Portland where she belonged with her friends and her job teaching at the dance school near her place. Although none of the things she had in her life back there brought much happiness, she would rather be there than here and it tore her apart to even think about her family again or specifically her father for that matter.

"Why did you even bump into me back in Portland? Were you stalking me? What were you planning on doing? Taking me out to dinner and then kidnapping me later?" Kim focused on her annoyance of what was happening to stop the pain she was feeling which she was unable to cope with that night.

"Of course not Kim." She was surprised to hear his voice close behind her but didn't turn around. "Firstly, we would've gone out to dinner." Kim sensed his body right behind hers; he took the hem of her shirt and began to lift it over her head.

She went along with it and held her cuffed hands above her head so he could slide off her top to expose her sports bra she had put on early that morning. She gulped when she felt his hands on her waist and his chest against her back.

"Maybe fuck a couple of times." He spoke soft and seductively, his lips dragging along her skin from her shoulder to her neck as he spoke.

"Then I'd take you on a weekend to D.C. where I'd bring you back to my boss."

He held her hands up again so that he was able to put on her matching care bear top. Kim did not welcome the feeling of fabric instead of his rough hands. She almost groaned but stopped herself when she felt his touch again. He leaned forward and reached his hands around to her wrists. Kim's breath hitched in her throat at his actions.

He tormented her skin, made her feel like everywhere he touched was burning. Nathan knew what he was doing to her, the affect he had on her. It made him want to test her patience even more but he stopped himself before he done something he would regret. His mission was to bring her to D.C. not sleep with her.

He surprised her even more with what he done next. Nathan unlocked one of Kim's hands and swiftly moved to her side to snap the open ring onto his other wrist. She looked in horror, unable to understand why he had made her believe for that one split second that he was going to free her hands. But instead of what she had hoped, he had made the situation worse by binding the two together between this metal.

"What the hell are you doing?" Kim narrowed her eyes at him in some sort of disgust, it made him chuckle.

"You think I'm going to let you escape when I go asleep? I don't think so. You won't find the key so there's no point in looking- besides, you can't go very far without me."

"But...But-" she was lost for words. God he was annoying, she thought. "But I need to pee?"

"Go ahead." He dragged her along into the bathroom and stood looking at the opposite wall, giving her as much privacy as he was willing to give.

"You can't be serious, I'm not peeing with you here."

"Well then I suggest you hold it in until morning." He remained facing the wall. He heard her let out an agitated sigh before shoving the lid up and going toilet. She slammed the lid down and flushed, making her way over to the sink to wash her hands. Kim dragged him with her; there were only a couple of centimetres of chain holding the two of their hands together so his hand was shoved into the sink along with hers.

"You're an idiot, you know that?" she gritted her teeth angrily at him once she saw him watching her, a smirk plastered upon his beautiful face.

Nathan said nothing, just made his way to the bed and got onto it on his side. Kim was forced to follow behind and stood there looking at him as he tried to get comfortable under the covers.

"How am I supposed to get into bed now that we're handcuffed?"

"Oh quit whining like a little child Kim." Nathan said before yanking her over the bed where she fell on top of him with a squeal.

She squirmed off of his body to lie on her side of the bed next to him, shooting him a deadly look to which he let out a hearty laugh. He already loved pissing her off, it was more than a little comedic.

"I bet you wish you had've said yes to that dinner invitation now don't you Kim?" he smirked, turning on his side to look at her adjusting in bed with the cuffs keeping them close.

"No! And you think I'd fuck you after one date?" Kim scoffed then narrowed her eyes at him in disgust when he gave her a wide grin.

"I know it sweetheart."

"Oh shut up!"

Chapter 5

"What the hell are you trying to do?" Nathan quirked an eyebrow at her.

The sight of Kim trying to pick the lock on the handcuffs that held them together with a hairpin immediately woke him up. He was barely awake two seconds before he turned over to find her trying to escape again. He rolled his eyes at her stupidity.

"Nothing." She seemed a little afraid at first, but then Nathan let out a sigh and rolled over, dragging her along with him. "Stop it!" she squealed in annoyance.

"Oh get over yourself Kim." He snorted. I barely even moved, he thought.

"Maybe I'll get over myself when you stop being such a dumbass and unlock my side of the handcuffs you fool." She huffed.

"I need a cigarette." Nathan whined and sat up. He fished around on the bedside table for the carton of cigarettes and grabbed his lighter. "You want one?" he mumbled as he held the stick between his teeth.

"Ew no... I'm a dancer, I need to stay healthy." Kim replied snobbishly. She felt the urge to cross her arms as she spoke but was unable to do so. She sat up like Nathan had done but turned her head slightly to look at him, awaiting a smart response.

"Aren't you a ballet dancer sweetheart?" he asked, his tone ridiculing. She knew exactly where this was going.

"Yes, and?" she asked sassily.

"And doesn't every little ballerina like you smoke?"

"That shit ruins your lungs, I need to be healthy to dance. I maintain my weight and stress levels healthily thank you very much." She was clearly offended by his question, it made him laugh a little.

"Suit yourself..." he lit up his cigarette and exhaled soft and slowly.

They sat in some strange silence for a while. Kim listened closely to their breathes while he puffed away on his cancer stick.

"Kim..." he started to talk again before her mind could begin to wander into the facts about the situation she was in right then. She turned her head again to look at his beautiful face- if only he wasn't a crazy kidnapper, she thought humorously to herself.

"Hmm." She murmured quietly, it was a sound Nathan oddly replayed again and again in his mind. It was gentle and warm.

"You need to understand that you're better off here with me, you're better off in D.C. where the CIA can take care of you."

"For how long? You told me I'm only being brought there because I'm in trouble and you're boss needs to question me. I'm not a fool Nathan, your mind games won't work with me. The only way any of you will be taking care of me is by slitting my throat after getting whatever information you need from me."

She was strangely calm, coming to terms with what was going to happen once they reached D.C. She knew those documents were extremely important and of great value to her father and his investors from Japan. The deal didn't fall through because of what she had taken back and she knew she would be in big trouble. All she needed to do now was find out what the CIA had to do with all of this.

"You don't know what you're talking about."

"Yes I do. I know how little value I am to you and your boss, considering he didn't care whether you brought me there dead or alive." Kim could have been making a valid point, if his lies about killing her were true. But they weren't, the CIA needed important answers from her and so her life was something Nathan needed to protect, or else he would end up dead too.

"We're leaving soon, you need to get ready."

He put his smoke out on the end table without giving it a second thought. The keys to the handcuffs seemed to appear in his hands out of nowhere in particular. He unlocked the cuffs and sprung up out of bed, for some reason Kim decided subconsciously to follow him.

He swooped the shower curtain to one side and gave her a wolfish smile.

"Hop in sweetheart we're showering together."

"You think you can get me naked that easily?" she rolled her eyes at him. "I don't think so-"

"Well I do."

Before she knew it she had taken two steps back in order to get away from his dark presence in front of her. But it was no use, her back hit the wall gently and he leaned down to place one of his hands on her cheek. He swiped his thumb over her soft skin and let out a low, wicked laugh that made her shiver in delight. She cursed herself for it and hoped he didn't notice.

Kim looked up at him, trying to keep her eyes glued to his in a deadly stare. She needed something to keep her mind off of how close he was and how intoxicating every part of him could be.

"I'm sure your mission wasn't to fuck me Nathan." She closed her eyes when she spoke. She had lost the battle to keep the intense eye contact they had been sharing because of the feeling of his other hand playing with the waistband of her bottoms.

"That's true Kimmy." Within a matter of seconds, he whisked himself away from her and moved to the other side of the room towards the door.

Kim was surprised, and... a little disappointed- that was what the insane side of her felt anyway. She tried not to let her annoyance show but it was written all over her face, clearly on display for Nathan to see. It made him chuckle cockily.

"Go shower Kim, we have places to be."

"Whatever." She grumbled.

"And if you are more than five minutes in there I'll be sure to come in and get you myself."

She wondered why that sounded so tempting.

Within an hour, Kim and Nathan had managed to get back on the road again. He had paid for the motel and hand-cuffed her before they went on their travels. It had seemed to Kim like they were on a road to nowhere. She watched gloomily out the window at the few cars that passed and the not-so-scenic fields that lay on either side of the road.

They had been driving for quite a while and had grown tired of sitting there doing nothing at all. She decided to turn to Nathan and examine every part of him visible to her. He intrigued her, to say the least. Despite the attraction she obviously had for him, she felt as though there was more to him that he wasn't telling her. Everyone had a story, she wondered what his might be. Kim was forced to share a car with him for however long it took to get to D.C. and she wanted to learn more about him.

"Kim stop staring at me." He hadn't taken his eyes away from the road when he spoke.

"I'm not staring, I'm just bored as hell."

"I don't care." He said monotonously. There was short silence before she spoke again.

"Want to play I Spy-"

"No."

"C'mon..."

"No." she rolled her eyes but set them back on him afterward. Kim noticed how he seemed eager to keep on going and how he griped the steering wheel with some sort of anxiousness. His eyes flickered countlessly between the road ahead and the mirrors for behind. It seemed as though he was waiting for something to happen and she wondered what that might be exactly.

"So- where are you from-"

"Kim we aren't making small talk or chatting each other up."

"Well you're no fun at all." She noticed how quickly he took the next exit and she furrowed her brows in confusion.

"Where are we going?" she asked.

"We're getting food and then we're heading off again." It took Nathan a couple of minutes to find a Drive Thru and after ordering for the two of them without asking Kim herself, he parked and began to eat his taco.

"I don't eat fast food." She stated. She had been partially lying. Sometimes, Kim would treat herself, but generally she liked to stay healthy and eat clean. It worked out better for her when she danced. She wondered when the next time she twirled in her satin pointe shoes would be.

"You haven't eaten since before I came to your apartment yesterday morning, you need to eat something."

"Before you broke into my apartment you mean."

"That's not the point, c'mon, you need to have something."

He was right; she did need to eat something. She was tired from her brain constantly going into overdrive with worrying thoughts and the fact that she was starving made it easy to give in and take a bite. Nathan quickly finished his food and rushed off to get back on the road again as she ate.

"You made short work of that taco sweetheart." he quirked an eyebrow at her once she had completely finished her meal. He seemed a little more relaxed than he was earlier.

"I said I didn't eat fast food, not that I didn't like it." He sniggered but nothing else was said for quite some time.

Kim fell asleep and Nathan kept on driving. He felt the urge to throw a blanket over her from the back seat but stopped himself. He decided when it was getting late that maybe it was time to find somewhere to stay and get some well needed rest.

Kim only woke up when Nathan finally found somewhere to stay. He shook her shoulder and she mumbled something before opening her eyes.

"Time to wake up sweetheart. We have to go inside."

"Mmm." She opened her door and got out of the car to walk next to him. She noticed the empty pool and how the water glowed in the darkness of the night.

They walked past it and took the stairs to the second floor. Nathan opened the door to their room and threw his bag on the ground. The bag that she had learned was filled with both his things and hers. He had packed it after he knocked her out yesterday morning with things she needed, even a toothbrush. She had called him a creep for going through her things once she found out but thanked him mentally for making sure she had everything she needed.

Nathan didn't dress her himself like he had done the night before. Instead, he uncuffed her and told her to get ready for bed while he went to the bathroom. Kim looked around the room and noticed the doors that led out to the small balcony.

Instead of getting changed like Nathan had told her to do, she wandered out onto the balcony quietly. She knew not to make a sound, a clear indication that the thought of escaping was fresh on her mind again.

Kim didn't know why she had forgotten about escaping until just then, all day she should have been looking for ways to get away from Nathan but not a single one had crossed her mind all day. She knew that what she had said to him in bed would be her fate. The CIA would most likely get rid of her once they had gotten what they wanted from her. Kim's blurry reality only made her gasp for air even more.

Her palms had become sweaty and she closed her eyes in hope to get some relief from the panic appearing before her eyes. What would happen when they reached D.C? What were they going to do to her? What were they going to ask her? She was afraid, the brave Kim was hiding on her and she didn't like it.

Kim gripped her clothes she was supposed to be changing into and thought of a plan. The swimming pool came into view as she stepped further onto the balcony over the railings that stopped her from falling off. She placed the clothes on the ground. Her hands were shaky as she gripped onto the cold metal and looked down to see the swimming pool just below her.

She decided her best bet was to jump, it was a jump she would definitely make. She threw her clothes down first, aiming for the ground rather than the pool. She would need something to get changed into once she soaked the ones she was in now. The clothes scattered on the pavement below but she managed to save them from the water.

Kim put one leg over the railings and braced herself for the jump into the water she was about to make. She was extra careful, making sure she didn't slip or fall. She took a deep breath and began to put her over foot over when Nathan's voice startled her.

"Kim?!"

Chapter 6

"Kim?!" She didn't see it but he jumped at the sight of her. What the hell was she trying to do?

Nathan didn't want to seem too interested and so his expression changed to a bored one. His shock was gone, he had realised by then that this was another attempt of an escape. He was just glad this one didn't involve her kicking him in the face or trying to make him crash his car.

"Don't step any closer or I'll jump." Her tone was panicked. He rolled his eyes at her words and how they sounded like a cliché suicide attempt.

"Do you actually think that if you jumped, I wouldn't find you? Even if you did manage to get away I would catch you sooner than you would think Sweetheart. So give it up, climb back over here to me and I'll dress you. It's clear you don't know how to do that yourself."

"Nathan this isn't a fucking joke okay!" she tried not to think about the fact that he was lacking a shirt and she could see every bit of skin on the upper part of his body. Kim really picked her times to be completely distracted.

"Kim, darling...Kim..." Nathan let out a small laugh at how crazy she was acting. "You know what? Why don't you just do it? Try and jump, we'll see how far you get." He crossed his arms, every part of him, inside and out relaxed. It made her rage on with fury, and so, she jumped.

As soon as her feet left the edge of the balcony, Nathan was running out of the room. He had the room key in his pocket and slammed the door shut. It took him only a couple of seconds to make his way down the stairs and out to the pool. Kim splashed around in the water and tried to compose herself to swim away from him but he was right in front of her, at the edge of the pool.

Her hands flailed around to stop him from going near her but without an difficulty, he scooped her up and out of the water.

"Get your hands off of me!" she smacked and slapped at him but he gave her no reply. He threw her over his shoulders and bent down to pick up the clothes she had thrown.

"Very clever Kim, trying to escape in a pair of Care Bear pyjamas? Are you fucking kidding me?" Nathan's voice dripped of annoyance, he wished he didn't provoke her to jump now and regretted the fuss it had caused.

"Stop touching my ass you pervert! I told you this yesterday." Kim warned but Nathan of course, listened to not a word she had said.

He carried her soaking body up the stairs and into their room again, slamming the door shut. He threw her with little care on the bed and kneeled down in front of her.

"Don't try to escape again. This is for your own good Kim. There CIA aren't the only ones out there looking for answers from you, but we sure as hell are the safer option. So I suggest you put up with me for the next few days and stop trying to run away because you're not going anywhere."

He was angry, frustrated and pissed off at that point. The fact that she refused to look at him only ticked him off even further. Kim was very aware of this, it was her ultimate goal.

"Look at me when I'm talking Kim."

She said nothing, she didn't respond in any way at all actually. She heard him grumble, then he roughly took her face in his hands, forcing their eyes to finally meet.

She didn't look pleased at all. Although it seemed like she hadn't listened to anything Nathan said, his words felt as though they were smothering her. She didn't know what to think or how to feel and it was the confusion that felt as though it was killing her slowly in that moment. When would everything be okay again?

"Get your hands off of me." The air around them had shifted and she noticed how daringly close he was to her. Kim wanted to tear her eyes away from him but she couldn't. Nathan knew what he was doing, he knew he had an effect on her and liked how she trembled in his arms at the sight of him there and then.

"Are you sure you want that sweetheart?" his voice was barely above a whisper, it was dangerous.

Nathan's hands moved slowly from her cheeks to her shoulders then to her waist where he played with her wet shirt. As he done this Kim moved her hands to press them on his chest, she was so close to pushing him away but couldn't find it in herself to do so just yet.

"Yes." She said weakly.

She wondered why she had even spoken at all, her words held no force or meaning, just lies. She wanted his hands to keep exploring her body, she needed him to keep on going until every part of her burned from his touch. Kim couldn't breathe when one of his hands reached the waistband of her trousers. She gulped and locked her eyes with his again, almost daring him to keep on going.

Kim didn't stop him once he moved closer to her and onto her legs. He pinned her down with his body and leaned his face just a breath away from hers. He pushed her wanting body to the point where she would allow him to do just as he pleased. Nathan knew this and with that, he quickly moved away , pulling on his t-shirt and snapping a handcuff on her wrist, the other on his own.

Kim felt nothing but raw embarrassment at that point. She grumbled to herself, annoyed that she could have been so stupid as to fall for his touch yet again.

"You know, you don't need to do that every time you cuff us together." She muttered. She wanted him, it was so blatantly obvious. That was why he continued to keep his efforts up of teasing her consistant over these past two days. He liked knowing he was in control, he liked knowing she wanted him.

"Why not? I like watching how you react to me." He whispered to her, making her shiver in complete delight despite not wanting to.

Within a second, he was close to her again. He cupped her cheek with one hand.

"Now I won't be able to get changed out of my clothes because I'm stuck with this thing on my arm and yours." Kim muttered, clearly distracted by the close proximity.

"I guess you'll just have to sleep in them tonight sweetheart." Nathan laughed gently but wickedly. His voice staying in that husky whisper that made her want him even more. She knew she wasn't thinking straight, she knew that for her to even consider allowing him to do anything to her was obviously absurd and irrational. "Or I could rip them off of you..."

Kim's mind went into overdrive once she heard the words escaping his mouth. She began to wonder what it would feel like to be with him. Her thoughts confused her, he confused her. Wasn't he supposed to be bringing her to D.C? Not trying to get her into bed. So why was he pretending he wanted this to go somewhere? She knew he wouldn't want her the way she wanted him right then. The rational part of Kim decided there and then that she would not react to him like this again though it was so difficult for her to stop.

It seemed as though her mind had been one step ahead of her body. Kim hadn't moved an inch away from him, she allowed him to hover over her and torment her neck with his lips. Nathan began to moved his body on hers, making her feel like she was about to turn to flames if he continued a minute longer. Her hands tangled in his hair, wanting to pull him away yet wanting to allow him to continue also.

He loved watching her responses, how she closed her eyes shut and exhaled deeply. It heightened his desire to take her just then although he knew he couldn't. He was supposed to be teasing her and not himself wasn't he?

"Nathan-" Kim couldn't help but moan his name aloud.

But her sane thoughts weren't what made her push him away, it was the sound of the door to their room being kicked off of the hinges that done the job.

Within a matter of seconds, the door fell loudly to the ground with a thud and four Japanese men entered. Kim shrieked in astonishment although Nathan seemed to deal with the surprise a little better.

He jumped up out of bed, dragging her up with him and began to ready himself for the four men nearing them with violent eyes. Nathan punched one continuously in the face until he fell to the ground but he knew the rest would not be that easy to take down. Two of the remaining three ganged up on him, punching and kicking vigorously while the last one moved to Kim.

She was surprised when he snatched her free arm up and examined it carefully. Her mouth was agape whilst the man pressed and pushed on her soft skin on the inside of her arm with his fingers, as if looking for something. But what exactly? He shouted something in Japanese to the other men but didn't get the chance to finish his sentence. By then, Killer Kim had kicked in and he examined her arm no more.

She grabbed her arm back from his reach and swiftly punched him in the face, a hit he definitely was not expecting. He recovered quickly and kicked her in the stomach. It hurt but not enough to stop her from continuing to fight back.

By then Nathan had managed to make the two men fall to the ground, the last one standing had hit Kim one too many times. She tried to block and hit back but he was the professional not her. She wished maybe she had picked up a tougher hobby than ballet, because she felt helpless as she blocked another punch he was throwing with her free arm.

Pure fury coursed through Nathan's veins at the sight of the toughest man left tiring Kim out. Nathan knew he was going to be the biggest challenge tonight. He began to fight back against the stranger in his rage but the man was too quick for Nathan. He head-butted Nathan before backing away and taking out a gun. Kim screamed but Nathan had recovered quickly and pulled her behind him.

The sound of the bullet pouncing out of the gun and into Nathan's left shoulder made Kim wince. He held her tightly behind him but then ran at the man before he could shoot again. Kim followed and noticed how quickly he had got the man between the two of them. He started to choke him with the chain of the handcuffs that tied them together. Nathan pushed the man forward into the metal chain. Kim watched, her eyes wide as the stranger struggled for breath. She couldn't believe she was helping Nathan to kill this man but didn't loosen her grip until the stranger had calmed down and fell limp to the ground.

Nathan took out his own gun then and walked to the bed to pick up the duffle bag. He handed it to her and continued to look around in case of any more unwanted guests.

"Take this." He said and pushed her behind him again. "Stay behind me Kim. No more fucking around, you do as I say or you'll end up dead." Nathan's tone was icy and serious.

Kim nodded, not saying a word as he led her quickly to the car. She gripped the duffle bag tightly and tried to calm herself down. They reached the car in no time and that was when Nathan fished around for the keys to the handcuffs. He unlocked the two of them. It was only then that he got a good look at her.

Kim was a little more than shaken up. Her eyes were like saucers, she shook involuntarily and her breathing was heavy. It was clear to him that she had never witness anything of this nature before, all of the trouble with her father's company must have only started after she left, he figured.

"Kim..." Nathan took a step towards her, her back was to the car and she was staring at the ground in a troublesome daze.

"Mmm?" her eyes hadn't moved despite him appearing in front of her.

"Kim we need to get going before someone else turns up."

"Yeah, okay." She whispered before entering through the passenger door. She needed to get a hold of herself.

And so they took off on their journey again, neither Nathan nor Kim uttering a word.

Chapter 7

"Who were those men back there?"

Kim had finally processed all of the events that had previously happened that night. It took her some time to finally speak, an hour had passed by the time she opened her mouth.

"Investors from your father's company." Nathan didn't take his eyes off the road as he spoke. He was on high alert, checking every few seconds in his rear view mirror to make sure no one was behind them.

"So they're working for my father? Why would they want to kill us?"

"They aren't working for your father Kim, more like he's working for them. The Japanese investors involved in the deal you stole the files from are powerful men. They want to take you back to Chicago to your father so you can fix what you've done."

Kim remembered five years previous and how she thought she had been doing a good thing. She would finally earn her father's complete approval after years of trying to make something of herself in the company. Her father had led her to believe she was making something very beneficial for the company and the investors, even her fiancé had convinced her to go ahead with the plans although she was more than apprehensive.

Despite how she felt about the whole thing, she began to make malware for computers her father's customers would use. She later learned that it would be used to steal important information from the U.S. government for the Japanese investors and as soon as she found this out, Kim stopped what she was doing. She knew she had made a huge mistake. Her father knew she was the only one he could trust that was skilled enough to create this specific, intricate weapon. And so when he found out she had pulled out of the job, he and the Japanese investors were not happy at all.

Kim immediately stopped working on the project once the penny dropped and she realised what her father wanted her to do. Someone else took had taken her place on the project. The person Kim thought she knew so well her entire life, the person she trusted and love- her fiancé. He too was a computer programmer and a good one too, but not as good as her.

Shane, her fiancé, had betrayed her. She had told him everything about the project the night she returned home after her discovery. Kim was an intelligent woman, she realised her fault and finally she had found out her father's true colours, although she had been ignoring it all along, she knew then there was no going back. She didn't want or need his approval for anything else in her life. She was done taking his orders and being tricked into his wicked and dangerous games.

Kim had decided she wouldn't allow her father to know that she had discovered his true plans but told Shane everything. He was someone she was extremely close to, she loved him after all and trusted him, too much. Shane went straight back to Kim's father and exposed her. Shane wanted in on the project and so continued on with the work what little work had left behind, she had destroyed everything she possibly could in order to make it difficult for them to continue on with the project.

Her father took all of the work she had spent weeks on and allowed Shane to completely take over. Although she knew that Shane would never be able to continue on or finish what she had started, she wanted to take back what was hers before she flew out to Portland to start fresh. Kim managed to get into her father's system in the company and take back what was hers before sneaking in to the main offices to retrieve any paper work so very little at all would be left behind.

Kim began to wonder how long Shane had decided he favoured her father over her. She couldn't help but think that their entire relationship was partially because he loved her but mainly because he wanted to get closer to her father. Maybe he asked her to marry him because he thought it might land him a higher spot in the company? Was everyone in her life, her friends too, influenced by her father and what they could get from her? It seemed so. Kim learned quickly that through the difficult times she faced, not a single friend remained loyal. No one came to visit her in Portland, no one called or texted.

"There's no way in hell that I'm going back to Chicago." Kim continued on with their conversation, her words came out steely and stern.

"I'm not sure you'll have much of a choice if they find you." There was a nervous silence for a moment. "I'm not the enemy Kim, I hope you'll understand that now."

She turned from looking out the window to him, her eyes full of scepticism. Nathan shot her a glance but then turned back to the road. Her eyes trailed from the stubble that crept onto his jawline to the bloodstained shirt he was wearing. It was then that she remembered he had been shot.

"Your shoulder." She was close to gasping but didn't want to seem like she cared that much. She leaned over in her seat. Kim was glad that he hadn't tied her up this time in the car. She went to place her hand near the wound but he hit it away.

"The bullet isn't too deep, I'll fix it up in the morning. For now, we need to get as far away from here as possible." Nathan brushed his injury off like it was nothing. He had learned to deal with bullets from a young age and the pain hadn't yet kicked in. It would take some time for the adrenaline to wear off inside of him.

"B-but it must hurt? You need to go to the hospital and get it fixed up."

"I'll be fine Kim, honestly." It sounded a little irritated then by her fussing. It made her regret ever saying anything at all.

Nathan sensed how she had become slightly wounded by his words and so, spoke again. "Just try to get some sleep, we'll sort everything out in the morning." He urged her, his tone gentler than before.

She nodded weakly before turning to look out the window at the passing darkness around them again. Despite her soaking clothes and troublesome mind, she fell asleep quickly.

"Nathan?" she mumbled quietly. She was still half asleep and wondering what she was doing standing up with her back to the car. "What the fuck Nathan?" she looked down and noticed he was undressing her.

"Oh shut up Kim, you think I need to wait until you're asleep to try anything with you? I'm getting you changed because you're wearing wet clothes. You were shivering in your sleep."

"Why not just wake me up then?" she questioned but allowed him to continue on. She stepped out of her trousers, one foot at a time.

"You don't think I tried? I spent five minutes shaking you but you wouldn't wake up."

"I can be a heavy sleeper sometimes." Kim felt a little embarrassed. "Don't look." She said.

She was still sleepy and her mind was slow at processing things but she knew he was taking off her underwear and she didn't know what to do. Nathan rolled his eyes and looked away, continuing to help her. He slid off her underwear and helped her step into new ones. Kim yawned as he glided her sweatpants up her legs. She placed her arms on his shoulders to steady herself.

"Ah Kim! Fuck!" Nathan winced in pain. "My fucking shoulder." He growled at her.

"Oh my god. I'm so sorry."

He stood back and threw her a baggy top that she guessed was his. She didn't question why she was going to wear his t-shirt instead of her own, just turned and changed out of her wet shirt into her new one. When she turned around, she saw Nathan pressing his hand down on the roof of the car, trying to compose himself.

"I need to get this thing out." He grimaced.

Kim's eyes widened at his words.

"Yourself?" she asked.

"No, I brought a doctor in the trunk with me. Didn't you see him when I put you in there? Of course I'm going to do it myself." Nathan grumbled.

"You don't have to be a bitch about it..."

"Just get in the car."

"But I thought you were going to take that bullet out of your arm?"

"Yes, I am. But I need to sit down."

Kim watched intently a couple of minutes later, close to looking away from the graphic scene unfolding before her eyes. Nathan rested the arm attached to the injured shoulder on the compartment between the two front seats. He was looking at his shoulder, trying to pick the bullet out for the past minute or two.

"Ahhh!" he grumbled with rage. His eyes were closed shut, his body trying to cope with the immense pain he was conflicting on himself. He looked away for a minute to take a breather. He almost had the bullet but needed to take a break. The pain was becoming too much to bear.

Kim felt sorry for him; she didn't want to see anyone go through this type of pain. Sure, she didn't particularly like this man but she had learned that he was the one who was supposed to be keeping her safe from those people the scary Japanese investors called on. She wanted him to be okay.

Nathan felt her soft fingers wrap around his free hand and squeeze it tightly. He turned quickly to look at her, blinking a couple of times. She looked nervous for what was about to happen and he could see her gulp. Their eyes met for the short silence that filled the car. Neither said a word for a moment and then Nathan began to take the bullet out again, squeezing her hand tightly as he done so.

He retrieved the bullet from his shoulder in a matter of seconds after his minute or so break. The relief of it was felt by not just himself but Kim too.

"Are you okay?" she asked gently.

"I'm fine." He said gruffly, he let go of her hand then and turned to set his eyes on the road ahead of them. Kim tried to brush off his indifferent gesture, she tried not to care and told herself to not be so soft the next time something like this was to happen. She had to continue to be tough, strong and brave Kim- not some sensitive and soft girl he could walk all over. He felt her touch too intense to take at that moment and needed a distraction from the shots of electricity that were going through his hand and arm where her touch lingered.

What the hell had he gotten himself into?

Chapter 8

"You need to go to the hospital Nathan." Kim was tired of saying it.

It had been two days since what happened and they hadn't seemed to bump into anymore strange men doing martial arts, yet. They stayed overnight in two nicer hotels but Nathan continued on with the journey despite how sick he had begun to feel. He was feverish and dizzy, he knew it wasn't the best idea to keep on driving but he wanted to just get Kim to D.C. and not have to worry about her for any more time than possible.

The past two days hadn't been filled with more of Kim's great ideas to escape, but instead with her constant nagging for him to go to the hospital. He said the wound would heal itself eventually but she didn't believe him.

"I'm not going to the hospital god damn it. I don't need to."

"Fine then, but don't come crying to me when your shoulder gets all septic and shit." He just rolled his eyes at her. "I'm being serious Nathan."

"Just- just be quiet okay?" he knew she was right but didn't want to admit it.

"Whatever. You know what's going to happen? Your shoulder is going to get all infected and you're going to die and then neither of us will make it back to D.C."

"I think I'd rather be dead right now than have to listen to your bullshit." He grumbled.

"You know what? I don't even care anyway. Maybe I would've been better off just going with those four men back there. I'd rather deal with their karate kung fu shit than have to sit here with you." Kim was giving as good as she was getting.

"Kung fu is actually Chinese Kim, not Japanese." He scoffed.

"Who the hell cares? I hope we wake up one morning and your arm falls off while it's attached to mine by the handcuffs you use. Then I'll be able to escape and leave you there, knowing I was right all along. You'd have to go back to your boss and tell him how I got away, minus an arm."

Without any notice given at all, Nathan swerved through two lanes and out of the first exit. Kim screamed when she was thrown around in her seat from the sudden jolting.

"Nathan are you fucking insane? What the fuck?" she questioned him, her eyes narrowed and her brows furrowed as he sped down the roads ahead of them.

"I'm going to the hospital to shut you up."

"No you aren't." she snorted, "You're going because you know I'm right and you also know that if you don't go, your arm is going to get infected just like I said it would."

"No, I'm right."

"I am."

"I am."

"Whatever." Kim rolled her eyes and relaxed into her seat a little. She turned her head and looked out the window.

Nathan allowed her to have the last word this time, in too much pain to keep on going with their bickering. He used his GPS to find the nearest hospital to him and within a couple of minutes, they were parking in the parking lot.

Kim was still in a huff and crossed her arms once she stepped out of the car. She followed Nathan inside where they would wait for an hour until there was finally a doctor free to see him. Kim and Nathan spoke very little in that hour while in the waiting room. After a couple of minutes, Kim had the urge to say something, anything at all, but just couldn't get any words out.

The doctor asked Nathan a few questions and examined his shoulder. He decided the best thing to do was to clean the wound thoroughly and give Nathan some medication to take home with him.

"How did this happen anyways? If you don't mind me asking..." the doctor spoke and turned around the find everything he needed to clean the wound. Nathan shot Kim a glance behind the doctors back to find she was already looking at him, her eyes widened slightly. His mouth turned into a smirk and she wondered what he was going to do next.

"I was trying to teach my girlfriend here how to shoot, she claims she accidentally shot me. But I don't think that's true, do you doc?" Nathan joked. He saw how Kim's expression blanched but she couldn't do or say anything because the doctor had already turned around to look at the pair of them. He chuckled warmly at Nathan.

"I'd like to think it is nothing but the truth." The doctor laughed and then told Nathan to pull down his sleeve and take off his shirt. He prepared himself to clean the wound and then spoke again. "You might need some moral support to get through this, I must warn you." He gave Nathan a sympathetic smile before looking over at Kim who had her arms crossed and her lips pursed. She was almost glaring at Nathan and didn't reply to the doctor.

"Well c'mon babe. Help me out here." He grinned wickedly at Kim, making her suppress a shiver.

She hated herself for feeling as affected by him- every part of him- as she was but it wasn't something she could turn on and off with the flick of a switch. Nathan was aware of this too, he liked seeing her squirm in the uncomfortableness and desire that he brought to her.

Kim knew the doctor was glancing between the two of them, wondering why there was so much tension between the couple. Why would this woman be the one who has clearly bothered when she supposedly shot him? Kim didn't want the doctor to think anything of the pair and so returned a smile to Nathan. He patted the examining bed he was sitting on, his legs dangling beneath him.

Kim jumped up on to the bed but kept some distance from Nathan. He winked at her and then placed his hand between her thighs, gripping the one closest to him and giving it a quick squeeze. Kim tried with much difficulty to stop herself from turning a bright shade of crimson but she was unsuccessful.

"Okay, I'm ready doc." Nathan turned and nodded at the other man.

Meanwhile, Kim was trying to catch her breath. His touch felt as though it would burn through her leg. She didn't think it had been possible until then, she never thought a man could make her feel that way. She knew next to nothing about him, she didn't want to know anything more either. She disliked him, he disliked her- so why was there a million thoughts running through her head in that instant? Kim understood it was an instant attraction, one that didn't seem to be dying down any time soon. She just hoped it wouldn't become stronger rather than weaken.

Kim gulped when she looked at him and saw how he winced slightly, his grip tightening ever so slightly on her thigh. It was then, she looked down and noticed all of the scars on his bare chest. Why hadn't she noticed before when he was shirtless? There was a sprinkle of healed bullet wounds on his torso, their scattered patterns made Kim look in bewilderment.

Everything was cleared up in the hospital room after thirty minutes. Nathan was given medication and advice to take in order to help the wound heal at the quickest pace possible. Kim had yet to speak once they were back in the car and on their way again.

"Why did you do that back there?" Was the first words to leave her mouth when they were settled in and driving at great speed down the highway.

"What sweetheart?" Nathan pretended he didn't understand her question.

"You need to back the fuck off, don't touch me again." She wondered why she was so afraid of him touching her again. Could it be that she felt like she couldn't resist? She hoped not but was still unsure.

"I feel like you're saying no but want to say yes." He laughed at her, causing anger to spark within her.

"Why do you think it's so funny Nathan? It's not."

"Because I find the whole thing quite humorous if you ask me." He came across as unphased, as always.

"The whole thing?" she questioned.

"You, and how affected you really are by me." He chuckled again to himself.

Kim knew she couldn't deny it, so instead let out a frustrated sigh and turned to look out the window. She would get him back another time- much sooner than he expected...

They arrived at their next hotel a couple of hours later. Kim began to wonder when they would get to D.C., they must have been half way there by then. Nathan unlocked the door to their room and looked around after stepping inside. The room was bigger than the others and decorated a lot nicer than previous places they had stayed at along the way.

Nathan walked over to the couch on the opposite side of the room and fell down onto it, sinking into the soft cushions. The duffle bag containing their things was at his feet and so Kim walked over to take her pyjamas out for the night. She was glad that yesterday, they had time to wash some of the clothes, her carebear pyjama set being one thing she definitely needed to clean. She took it from the bag and began to walk to the bathroom with her things.

"Don't be too long in there, or else I'll have to come in and get you." He warned her but remained relaxed with his eyes closed, his hands behind his head.

"Whatever." She called back.

She quickly got changed and had suddenly come up with a plan at the sight of Nathan so relaxed on the sofa. This was the most laid back she had saw him before. His eyes were still closed and his legs were open. A wide grin fell on Kim's face once she spotted him.

Kim tiptoed quietly towards the sofa, still unnoticed until she placed her hands on both his thighs. She knelt down on the soft carpet beneath her and found it strange when he didn't respond or even jump at her actions. She began to gently run her hands up and down his thighs. It was then that he finally spoke.

"What are you doing Kim?" Nathan had yet to open his eyes. He wondered where this was going but wanted to show lack of interest.

"You'll see." She almost giggled, slowly moving her hands to his zipper and undoing his button.

"I thought you didn't want me to touch you ever again." His mouth turned upward to form a small smile but he didn't open his eyes. He paid close attention to Kim's roaming hands, not being able to help himself.

"That doesn't mean I can't touch you." Her voice was low and sultry. She unzipped his pants and placed her hand on his manhood, the thin material of his underwear being the only barrier. She almost thought she heard him groan aloud at her actions but was unsure.

"Kim..." he said aloud, this time she knew she wasn't imagining it. She had taken him into her hand and by then, he couldn't help but open his eyes to look at her. She grinned at him when she saw the complete lust and desire behind his blue eyes.

"Shh." She spoke gently, moving her face closer to his body. She was tempting him, and he found it extremely difficult to not pick her up then and have his way with her. That was what they both clearly wanted. But instead, he done what he was told and kept his mouth shut. He could feel her soft breath on him and put his head back again, squeezing his eyes shut.

She was so daringly close to him. He needed her then, awaiting her touch patiently, but it only led to disappointment when she took her hands away and stood up from the floor. Within a second, Kim was walking briskly away from an unravelled looking Nathan sitting on the sofa. She was smiling to herself as she got into bed, knowing her plan had worked.

"Kim? What the fuck Kim?" Nathan fixed himself and stood up to look at her.

His brows were furrowed and his features held an annoyed expression until she began to laugh out loud at his exterior. Then he looked a little shocked and taken aback.

"What Nathan?" she asked sweetly, she was acting innocent and this pushed his anger further.

"What the hell was that just there? You- you can't just do that."

"I was just making sure-"

"Making sure what?" he raised his voice although she remained calm as she moved under the covers on top of her.

"You're as affected by me as I am by you." She grinned at him and spoke in a matter-of-fact tone that aggravated him.

"No I'm not." He denied it but knew that there was a small chance that he was going to be able to talk himself out of this argument. She would come out on top and he just knew it.

"Yes you are. Nathan- there's no denying it now. You would've gladly let me put your dick in my mouth just a minute ago, you were waiting for me to do it and now you're angry because I didn't." Kim was turned on her side, her head propped up on her hand as she looked at him. Her statement was the truth and nothing but the truth. Nathan knew he could deny it no more.

"You know Kim, you have a beautiful way of putting things." he said sarcastically. She could tell he was pissed, and it amused her.

"I know." she grinned back at him.

"You're such a bitch." He huffed out before stomping into the bathroom and slamming the door behind him.

She called into him, knowing he would hear her and be irritated even more.

"I know!"

Chapter 9

"Kim, we need to get out of here. Right now."

Those were the first words she heard that night. Nathan was shaking her in order to wake her. She could be a heavy sleeper at times and so he was finding it a difficult task to do.

"God damn it Kim. Do you want a repeat of a few days ago when those men stormed the place with their karate kung fu shit?" Nathan had grown irritated very quickly, considering she had yet to make a move to get up and they had such a limited amount of time.

"You said Kung fu wasn't Japanese." She grumbled, not sure whether this was reality or a dream. She hoped it was the latter. She was in no mood to fight off scary Japanese men again.

"There's no time for fucking around Kim. Get up."

It took Nathan two seconds before he ripped her out of the bed and threw her over his shoulder. All of a sudden, she was awake and alive. She squealed and hit his back repeatedly but he didn't put her down, only grabbed the duffle bag and his keys. He checked around the room in case he had left something behind and then went on his way down the stairs to the car park.

Kim didn't kick up a fuss about where Nathan's hands where, or how she wanted to get down. She just let him carry her; unable to process fully the fact that someone else was after them. As he put her down, the noise of a car screeching nearby caught her attention and she looked in horror as a black van raced towards them. She began to scream but Nathan soon cut her off.

"Get in the car!" he yelled before pulling out a gun and firing it at the tires on the car.

Kim did as she was told and waited anxiously for him to follow her. It was less than a minute later, Nathan had stopped firing his gun and jumped inside then, throwing the duffle bag on her lap before starting up the car. He rushed down the road and shot out the window at the same time, aiming at the van behind them.

It was beginning to slow down because of the punctured tires but kept going until it could drive no more. Nathan focused solely on the road then, continuing to check in the rear-view mirror every couple of seconds to make sure no one else was behind them. Kim felt she was gasping for air, while trying to figure everything out and stay calm at the same time- a task that was extremely difficult for her to do right then.

Nathan noticed her distressed state and looked at her out of the corner of his eye a couple of times. She was trying to stop herself from shaking, she didn't want to seem weak, she didn't want to look like a victim. It took her a short time to adapt to the aftermath of the last attack they had on them, she just needed a little quiet time to register everything in her mind.

"Kim you need to relax. They're gone for now, everything is going to be okay."

"Is it though?" Definitely not, she thought to herself, answering her own question.

It was still dark out and she could see very little from her window on the passenger side of the car. She still examined the outdoors while Nathan eyed her with consideration. He let out a sigh and continued on driving.

"How long will it take us to get to D.C?" Nathan was surprised by her question. It almost felt like she wanted to go then?

"A couple more days."

"Okay." Kim croaked out. It stirred something inside of him, something that felt a lot like sympathy but he tried not to dwell on it. He shrugged it off and continued on driving.

After an hour or two on the road, Nathan decided to stop off on the side of the empty roads to stretch his legs. He was tired from lack of sleep and one of his colleagues calling him to warn him of the men hot on their tail. Nathan's moving around in the car woke Kim from her light sleep she had just fallen into only minutes ago. She looked at him with a grim expression still plastered on her face.

"Let's get some air." He said before unbuckling his belt and stepping out of the car.

The sky had begun to brighten and the air was crisp when it hit her. She took a deep breath and sat down at the side of the road, looking out at the shadows of trees in the forest in front of her. While her eyes focused on the beautiful landscape off in the distance, the sun rising perfectly on all of the trees, Nathan changed out of his pyjamas. No one was around and she hadn't turned her head while he was changing.

"Maybe you should get dressed too." Nathan said as he sat down beside her.

"No, I'm good. I might sleep in the car for a little while when we get back driving." Kim's voice was soft, he almost thought it was sweet. He could tell by the calmness of her tone that she was obviously very tired.

"Suit yourself." He got comfortable on the dusty ground of the deserted road.

"Are they going to keep coming after us Nathan?" Kim didn't want to sound scared but she couldn't help it. The seriousness of this situation was beginning to dawn on her more than ever before. It was almost making her regret everything she had done to get justice for herself back in Chicago.

"Yes, but don't worry about it. I'm going to get you back to D.C. I never fail to get a job done."

"Why don't we just fly there? Why is it just you? Wouldn't it be safer if there were more people involved-"

"I work alone." He butted in eagerly, his voice held some kind of anger that Kim found strang. The harshness of his tone made her turn her head to look up at him.

"W-why?" There was a long pause after her question. She wondered whether he was going to answer it at all or choose to ignore it. Nathan was trying to decide if letting her in on this subject would be a good choice or not. It startled him a little- the thought that he was even considering telling her about his life.

"I always have. It's my one rule since I started working with the CIA."

"How long have you been working there?" Kim was curious. She was still looking at him but his gaze had settled somewhere in front of them.

"Since I'm eighteen. Everyone has been involved in the agency for generations in my family."

"So your mother and father are both agents too?" she noticed how he flinched at the mention of his parents. She wondered if she had asked too much too quickly, would he be angry with her?

"They both passed away when I was sixteen." The words were difficult to say as they left his mouth. He was confused as to why he had even told her that information anyway, maybe it was because of how tired he was.

"I-I'm sorry to hear that."

She felt terrible for even mentioning them, although Nathan came across as a man of little emotions, the death of a mother or father was certainly a catastrophic event that would definitely change a person's life forever. She didn't want to bring it up unless he was comfortable with talking about it. Nathan noticed her discomfort. Despite having dealt with the fact that his mother and father were both dead, there were things that had not been buried with them. Justice was not done for either of his parents- yet.

"Let's not talk about them anymore." He decided it would be better for both of them to talk about a different topic.

"Okay." Kim's voice was just above a whisper. She nodded slowly in agreement with him and a short comfortable silence fell between the two for a couple of minutes until she felt like speaking again.

"You know, if I thought all of this would've happened from what I done when I was twenty-one, I think I would have reconsidered my options." Kim smiled sadly, looking at the forest in front of them again.

"Why did you do it in the first place? Why steal from your own father's company?"

"Nathan I told you already-"

"Why did you take something from your father that you knew was important?" he rephrased his question.

"I-I guess I just realised what my life had become. I was sick of saying yes to everyone around me to keep them happy, finally saying no felt so liberating. I can't explain it. I made a bad decision, I was tricked into agreeing to make something for my father and his Japanese investors and when I realised this I backed out of the project and took back all of the files, everything I had created to stop them from reaching their goal."

"So you didn't know that the software or malware you were creating was going to be used in order to steal information from customers and the U.S Government?" Nathan questioned bluntly, not believing her at all.

"No, I didn't think it would be used for something that serious." She was telling the complete truth yet Nathan wasn't convinced. He eyed her with inquisitiveness.

"But didn't you think about it while you were working through the project that maybe it would be used for bad rather than good. The production of such things would never be seen as good anyway- whether it was linked with the government or not." Kim understood what he was saying. She felt foolish because of his words, because it seemed so clear to him and even her now- but at the time things were different.

"There was a time when I would have done anything for my father. For his approval. For him to consider me as a someone, a great and powerful person just like him. I know it's difficult for you to believe me, it's hard for even me to believe myself now, but I was so blinded by my father's lies and my obsession with seeking approval that I believed back then, the project would benefit the company and the investors. I didn't understand the true motive behind it all until later on when I discovered it myself. My father was lying to me and I allowed that to happen so I suppose I need to take responsibility for my actions." Nathan didn't know why, but he felt her words were the truth. He would never tell her that though.

"As soon as I realised what was going on around me, with the project, the investors, my father, hell my whole family and friends- I backed out of everything. I took back all of the files and all of my work I could take and destroyed every piece of it. I didn't want them to continue on with what they were trying to do and wanted to make it hard for them to achieve their goals without any of my work to help them."

"But it didn't matter, they found someone else for the project." Nathan added.

"Yes, they did..." she hesitated. She wondered if Nathan knew who exactly it was that continued on with the project. "My fiancé." Her words made him look at her in all of the bewilderment he was allowing her to see, which was very little but enough for her to realise he didn't know the man who took over was someone very close to her.

"Shane Parker is your fiancé?" he narrowed his eyes at her.

"Was. That bastard's nothing to do with me anymore." Kim corrected him. "The name Kim Parker wouldn't have suited me anyway..." Kim added humorously.

"But why?" Nathan didn't understand. Kim had sounded like somewhat of a man-hater from the beginning when he first met her, but he understood now her reasons behind it.

"Because Shane loved my father. He wanted power and status within the company, I guess he needed that more than he would ever need me..." Although she sounded and looked pathetic by what she was saying, she couldn't help it- or the tears that welled in her eyes the moment the words left her mouth. She blinked them away quickly as to not let any of her emotions show in front of Nathan who was trying to work this girl out right then. She was an intricate puzzle, ruined by betrayal and lies. He wondered whether it was a good idea to try and solve her or not, everyone was messed up- even himself.

"That's what people want Kim. Power and status are more important than love." Nathan spoke truthfully and bluntly to Kim, his words awakening a strange cocktail of anger and agreement within her.

"I trusted my father, I trusted my brothers and I trusted Shane. I even told him about my discovery and how I was planning on moving after ruining the project. I took all of the trust I had put in my deceiving family and put every last bit of it into the one person I thought truly loved me. The one I would go home to after every shitty day, the one I could confide in, the one that didn't need convincing of my value. He was supposed to love me no matter what- despite everyone else deciding I wasn't good enough- he reassured me day after fucking day. I put my faith in him, I trusted him with everything I was saying because he was supposed to understand but he didn't. Shane lied to my face and then went back to my father and told him every god damn thing I had trusted him with." Kim took a breath. She knew she would regret telling Nathan anything at all later one but thought that if these were her last few days, depending on what the CIA done with her, she wanted to get a few things off her chest.

"You can justify Shane's actions because of the importance of power all you want. I get it. You're an asshole, like every other man I've come across." She spoke her last few words with a matter-of-fact tone.

Her speech had pushed Nathan in the direction that her story was more truth than lies yet he didn't want to believe it. He was so used to seeing the story in a different way when being told by his co-workers and by doing his research that Nathan didn't want all of his preconceptions to be false. Everything he had thought about Kim's situation would be completely wrong if what she was saying was true.

Since he started on the case, he had thought of her as a conniving, scheming, selfish person who wanted everything to be her way- that was why he thought she had ran away with the files from the project in order to start something from her father's idea herself. He had imagined her as an intelligent and ruthless human being. He even thought of her as evil but since they had first met, he began to think the story he had taken from everything he learned about her situation could be nothing but lies.

"But I don't mind if you're an asshole or not. I don't expect much more. Once you get me to D.C safe and sound I don't give a crap." Kim spoke gently, coming to terms with the words that were leaving her mouth. She let out a deep breath and rested her head on Nathan's shoulder, admiring the view in front of her amongst the quietness that surrounded them.

Sometimes there were the virtuous among the sinful. But it was difficult for Nathan to face the reality that with bad there was also good- it always had been a struggle for him.

Chapter 10

"Ah, fuck." Nathan muttered under his breath before continuing to shave his jawline.

After failing to shave his face with his left hand because of his shoulder, Nathan tried using his right hand but was doing a terrible job. He didn't understand why, but this morning his shoulder hurt more than it had before over the last few days. Nathan was left handed and so wasn't used to using his right hand. He found it unbelievable that with every try, he managed to cut himself. It was becoming more frustrating with each attempt.

Kim should have been getting dressed for the day ahead of them, but instead she stood on the other side of the closed bathroom door, listening intently. She had always been a nosey person.

"Fuck!" He grumbled in anger before she heard something being thrown inside the bathroom.

"Nathan?" Kim called quizzically; she wanted to know what was going on in there and what was taking him so long.

"What?" he snapped from behind the door.

"I need to brush my teeth, are you nearly finished in there? Can I come in?" her voice was soft and quieter than usual. For a moment, she had sounded as though she was making an attempt at being nice to him. But that didn't last long.

"Yes." He grumbled.

She almost burst into laughter at the sight of a very pissed off looking Nathan gripping the edges of the sink in front of him. He was shirtless, half his face was covered with shaving foam and there was blood dripping from some parts of the skin on his face. Her eyes wandered from him to the razor thrown on the countertop.

"What?" He barked at her once he noticed she was trying to supress her laughter.

"So that's what has you so cheesed off." She ignored his aggravation and smirked at him before jumping up to sit on the countertop right beside the sink.

Kim noticed how his expression softened a little, as if he could've laughed at the situation but forced himself to stop. She swung her legs and continued to look at him, waiting for a reply. Nathan pinched the bridge of his nose, unsure as to whether he was annoyed at Kim or himself for finding the whole thing funny too.

"Kim, your statement could be laughable but not because it's funny, because you're funny. And not like haha let's laugh together funny, I would be laughing at you, not with you if I wasn't in such a bad mood."

"In what way?" she asked in a smug tone, quirking an eyebrow at him.

"Look at you. A twenty six year old sitting on a countertop with Care Bear pyjamas on wondering why I'm so cheesed off... I'm just two years older than you and I haven't used that term since elementary school."

"You're two years older than me and you can't even shave your face." Kim retorted.

"You're unbelievable." He sighed, making her giggle. It was a strange thing for Nathan to hear from her, it stuck out in his mind, bounced around his brain like an echo and made him want to smile.

"Oh boy, your panties are really in a twist." She continued on, receiving a glare from him.

Kim rolled her eyes and then picked up the razor lying near her. She tapped it against the basin of the sink and whisked it around in the water for a minute to clean it out.

"Come here." Kim said gently, all jokes aside then.

She felt sorry for him for some strange reason. Nathan hesitated, his eyes quickly connecting with hers. A silence full of tension filled the air before he decided to take the first step towards her. Neither spoke for quite some time. Nathan walked between her legs and allowed her to run the razor over his skin with ease.

She tipped his chin upward a couple of times to get at all angles, all the while he was watching her carefully- readying himself for her to slit his throat at any moment. The razor glided over his jaw smoothly. He noticed how her brows furrowed in concentration. It was just a couple of minutes before she was pressing the damp towel he had put aside over his clean-shaven face. By then, the cuts he made had stopped bleeding. Kim patted another dry towel over his face that was only centimetres away from hers. She had been avoiding eye contact the entire time but couldn't shy away from it anymore.

"Now." She almost whispered with finality once she looked him in the eye.

She examined his face quickly, he seemed to be distracted. Kim thought it was the perfect time to get him back for all he had done in the previous days of their trip together. She noticed him leaning in and staring fixatedly at her lips. She allowed him to keep on going until his eyes were closed and his lips were almost touching hers. It was then that she moved to the side to avoid him and hopped down off the counter.

"You need to hurry the hell up." Kim acted as if nothing had happened. She smacked him on the behind before saying "Go get dressed cranky pants." And with that she headed out of the bathroom, a grin plastered widely on her face that he could not see. She closed the door behind her, leaving him staring at the handle.

That girl would be the death of him, he thought.

"So, ballet huh?"

"I thought you said no small talk." Kim retorted.

A conversation seemed like something on the cards for both of them, considering they had been driving for a couple of minutes already and had barely said two words to each other. Nathan seemed to have been brooding quietly about the bathroom incident for quite some time. She found it hilarious but refrained from telling him so. She watched him carefully out of the corner of her eye, until he had decided in his own head that he would get her back sooner than she thought.

"Fine then..." he sighed.

He was finding it extremely difficult to stop the want he had from showing. He wanted to get to know her and that was a bad sign. She engrossed him without doing very much at all. For one to go from working in one of the world's best technology companies to ballet seemed like a strange change to make.

"I started when I was four and fell in love with everything about it." Kim stated, smiling to herself from the memories that came flooding back to her. "I gave it up for a while, my father wanted me to focus on the company and so I obviously did what he said."

She tried her best not to sound like she was seething but couldn't help it. She was angry at her father of course, but most of all herself for being so foolish.

"Did you enjoy working for your father's company? Or was that another thing he pushed you to do?" Nathan was still trying to figure her out, still trying to sift through her story to find holes.

"I was interested in computers and the company since I started high school. That was something I didn't need en-couragement from my father for. But as I began moving up in the ranks, I found that I had little time for ballet or other things that were separate from the company. Even Shane was working there and so my life seemed to suddenly be based around the company and my father only."

"I'm sure being a part of the company wasn't your main passion in life if you felt that way about it."

"It's just- I don't know... I felt like my life had been planned out for me by everyone else. I felt like I had fallen into some kind of trap, my life was working out but it didn't feel right. S ure... I had money and power in a world renowned company, but at the same time it seemed to not be working out. I know it sounds confusing, but it was difficult for me to process too. I felt brainwashed, like I had been told to like the life I had so I did until of course I finally snapped out of it."

"Do you think that was a good decision?" Nathan wondered, clearly interested. She was surprised by his curiosity and took some time to think about his question.

"I'm not sure. Now I'm sitting in a car with some dumbass from the CIA- and that's not even half of the problem." She replied, a hint of humour in her voice.

"So Shane huh?" his words caused her to chuckle, he looked at her then and wondered what she had found funny.

"Is that how you bring everything into a conversation? 'So ballet huh?' 'So Shane huh?'" she imitated him. He cracked a smile which made her feel strangely rewarded.

"I guess it is."

"Why do you want to know about Shane?"

"Is it a touchy subject?" he answered her question with another question. He knew that way he would get an answer from her somehow.

"No." Kim replied quickly. "Shane was a big part of my life for a long time, but I told you already what he did and how I felt about it. I'm over it." She felt as though there was a small part of her that hadn't fully gotten over it and that she was lying to Nathan slightly. There was more to her story than she had told him, a key element was missing that she had purposely left out to avoid further humiliation at how much of a train wreck her life was back then. She wasn't good enough for anyone in her life back then, not even herself. But things were different now, she thought. She valued her opinions of herself over other's.

"Men are bastards, I understand that now."

"Not all men Kim."

Nathan seemed a little defensive, he felt like it too but why? He knew he was most likely worse than any of the men that were previously in Kim's life so why did it matter anyway? She rolled her eyes, causing him to squint at her.

"What?" He asked.

"You're a liar."

"Whatever."

There was a short silence in the car before she decided to change the topic. She didn't want to focus all her energy on the terrible past that haunted her every day now.

"So the CIA huh?" she mimicked his voice and nudged him with her elbow as she spoke.

"What about it?"

"Is it something you always wanted to be a part of?" Kim didn't want to mention his parents and was trying desperately not to bring them up by accident.

"Yes." He replied then hesitated for a moment. "My mom and dad were agents too and I always wanted to be like them." She felt as though that small sentence took a lot of courage to speak aloud.

"I see." She gave him a small smile but he hated it. She was reacting like everyone else- trying to give him sympathy that he didn't want or need.

"Cut it out Kim." He said, his voice cold and reserved.

"Wha-"

"I don't need you to feel sorry for me, so please don't try."

"I-" Kim didn't know what to say, she couldn't help but feel a kind of sadness in herself from hearing of both Nathan's parents passing away when he was young. "Okay." She nodded at him, trying to search her brain for another question to ask to change the subject. "Don't you get bored of all this spy bullshit and running away from people?"

"I'm not a spy Kim, I'm an agent." He scoffed, clearly not holding a grudge against her for sympathising with him. She as glad.

"Well yeah, whatever..."

"I enjoy it, as long as I'm working on my own. It can be quite thrilling at times, I'm always looking for an adrenaline rush. Plus getting to the bottom of things and getting justice for crimes done by people like your Dad is kind of rewarding."

"Nathan."

"Yeah?" he asked, looking at her for a moment then diverted his eyes to the road again.

"Please don't call him my Dad again, call him my father. It sounds more appropriate."

Kim wasn't comfortable with the word Dad still. A dad was a man who raised you, who cared for you and your feelings.

Someone who would look out for their daughter, who would protect them and support them no matter what. A dad was a man who cared and loved unconditionally. Kim hadn't got a dad for a very long time, she had lost him many years ago.

Chapter 11

It seemed to Nathan that Kim had been particularly lively and cheerful that day in the car. After they both talked for some time, he drove them to a restaurant. Kim was delighted that it wasn't a fast food one. She had smiled a lot that day, he even did a couple of times too. They talked and shared and talked again.

Nathan was still trying to figure her out. Even after a day of learning new things about her, he felt he shouldn't trust everything she was saying. People could lie quicker than one would like to think. There was a part of himself that wanted to find gaps in her stories, a part that wished he didn't want to believe her so quickly. But Nathan soon found he couldn't help it anymore.

They had found somewhere to stay and were settling in for the night. Nathan was getting ready for bed when he spotted Kim sitting on the countertop in the bathroom beside the sink. It was like a replay of earlier that morning when she shaved his face for him except they were in a different hotel.

The memory made him reach up and touch his clean-shaven jaw.

"What are you doing?" he poked his head in through the doorway.

Kim was sitting with her legs swinging beneath her, wearing a familiar t-shirt. She seemed to be in deep thought but snapped out of her daze once she heard him speak.

"Nothing..." she replied quietly, knowing what his next question would be.

"Is that my shirt?" he quirked an eyebrow at her, a shadow of a smirk appearing on his lips. He was fully in the bathroom by then, almost standing in front of her.

"Maybe."

"Take it off." He said, not being completely serious.

"No. I have nothing else to wear."

"Did you just take that out of the duffle bag while I wasn't looking?" he chuckled, making her stomach flutter.

"Yes." She replied quickly, trying her best not to be embarrassed.

"That's my last clean one left Kim, take it off."

"No... We need to clean our stuff again. I'm running out of things to wear."

"So you've decided to steal my clothes until then?"

"Oh shut up." She grumbled. He had finally made his way to stand in front of her, his presence almost making her tremble. She reached up and played with the collar of his t-shirt, not looking him in the eye when she spoke again. "How's your shoulder?" her voice was gentle. He felt like she really did want to know the answer, like she genuinely cared.

"Not as sore as it was this morning."

"I reckon you were pretending just so I would shave for you- so you could get closer to me of course." She looked up then, staring into his blue eyes. He was closer than she had expected.

"I didn't ask you to do that, so maybe you offered because you're the one who wanted to get closer to me." He laughed a little but was then distracted by her lips.

"I don't think so." The pair's lips were almost touching then, they both looked up from the other's mouth so that their eyes met.

"Well I do." Was the last thing said by either before their lips met for a slow and sultry kiss. Although soft and relaxed, it was electrifying. There was some need behind it, some hunger coming through on Nathan's part.

Kim brought her hands up to tangle in his hair once he licked her bottom lip for entry. He bit her lip lightly before his roaming hands reached the bottom of her shirt, or his shirt to be more exact. They broke away for a split second in order for him to undress her, leaving her in just her under-wear. His breathing was rapid, his blood coursing through his veins. There was no denying the fact that both had a strong attraction for the other.

Nathan's hands ran across her skin to undo her bra then. Her breath hitched in her throat once his mouth moved from her neck down to her chest. She pulled him away after a minute or two so she could kiss his lips again. As she did so her hands went to the waistband of his bottoms. Nathan had been thinking very little until then, her touch seemed to wake him up from his day dream, from his want to have her.

Nathan found it difficult to do, but pulled away from her lips slowly. He placed his hands on either side of her head to stop her from what she was doing. Nathan took a deep breath before he spoke.

"Kim." He said breathlessly, making her look into his eyes then.

"What?" Her voice was barely above a whisper. She didn't want to stop and so went in again to kiss him but it didn't last for long.

"We can't do this." He said, his eyes closed shut. He had one last ounce of restraint left inside himself to allow those words to leave his mouth. Nathan knew the sparks inside him were the same on her part and he wanted nothing more than to be with her in that moment but he couldn't.

"Why not? It's just sex Nathan." She spoke bluntly, getting more than a little frustrated then.

"Because- Because I don't want to." He lied causing her to pull away completely from him.

"You know what? I'm getting sick of your fucking games Nathan. You're saying no but every other part of you is saying yes. Don't act like this is one sided." She was pissed off, more than he expected. But this wasn't another game to him, he had just managed to snap back into reality at the right time. Or maybe the wrong time.

"I'm not playing around this time Kim, we just can't okay?"

"Whatever." She said shortly before grabbing his discarded t-shirt and covering herself. She stomped out of the bathroom to find the duffle bag.

"Kim..."

"What?" she called over her shoulder to him as she picked up her Care Bear pyjamas out of the bag.

"You said it yourself, I was sent to bring you back to D.C, not to fuck you. If we did do anything- it would complicate things." He watched as she dressed herself in her dirty pyjamas and threw his shirt back into the bag. She was even more irritated then, because she knew what he was saying was right. But Kim also knew what she wanted, and that was him.

"I get it." She seemed to be a little calmer when she spoke this time. She walked around to her side of the bed and got in.

"You can wear my shirt if you want, I'll wear a different one tomorrow."

"It's fine." Kim replied quickly. He had to laugh aloud at her behaviour although he knew she wouldn't approve.

"Kim. C'mon..." She didn't say anything else, only get settled into bed.

She knew she was being childish, but she couldn't help how she felt. Being humiliated again by him was something she promised wouldn't happen. She felt embarrassed by what had happened in the bathroom just minutes ago and what was troubling her most was that she still couldn't shake the strong attraction she had for Nathan.

Nathan understood she probably wasn't going to budge, she was stubborn and he understood that. He was the same sometimes too. He wanted to reassure her that whatever there was between them wasn't one sided. He was unsure as to why he even cared about her feelings then, but couldn't help it.

He got into bed beside her and turned off the lamp on the bedside table. Then, he took the handcuffs and felt around for her hand. He caressed the skin on her wrist gently before snapping the metal shut. He turned to face her but she had her eyes shut, faced towards the ceiling. Nathan took a moment to take in her facial features, she looked so relaxed. He was quite surprised when she finally opened her mouth to speak.

"I'm sorry, I just overreacted." Her eyes didn't open when she spoke.

"Kim-"

"It's fine, I get it. Say no more." Kim was definitely swallowing her pride in order to apologise, it was a big deal for her and he guessed that too.

"But-"

"God damn it you're irritating." She said calmly, letting out a deep breath. She let out a small laugh then at herself and turned to look at him in bed.

"Not as irritating as you." He retorted, laughing a little himself too.

"Whatever." She got comfortable on her side and then looked at him. He was already staring at her. Once their eyes met, he reached out to run his fingers through her hair and over her temple a couple of times, making her gulp. The action relaxed her and she sighed out loud, closing her eyes again.

"I just don't want to make things complicated- for everyone's sake." She had to deal with his words, although staying away was not something she particularly wanted to do. She knew he was right and so she nodded.

"Okay." Kim whispered as he played with her hair, putting her to sleep quicker than she had the past couple of nights. "Goodnight Nathan." She added gently before falling into a deep sleep.

"Goodnight Kim." He said softly, but she was already asleep.

They had been driving all day and the sun was beginning to set over the cloudless sky. Neither had spoken about the night before or how strange it was for the two of them to be so nice to each other. The familiar bickering had continued throughout the day, but something was different.

Kim noticed Nathan had been a lot more on edge the next day, she found it quite hard to believe he was the same person that had played with her hair until she fell asleep the night before. He was on and off his phone a lot during the trip and when they stopped off for something to eat but he wouldn't tell her what the matter was. She thought it might have been that more men on her father's side were coming for them again but he reassured her that that wasn't the case.

"You are such a stick in the mud Nathan, honestly."

"Because I won't play eye spy with you? You're being ridiculous."

"Fuddy-duddy." She retorted to which he replied with a scoff.

"You're just proving my point."

"Grouch."

"Crybaby."

"I spy with my little eye something beginning with a."

"I told you already we aren't playing eye spy."

"No, that doesn't start with a..." Kim ignored his sentence. "Do you give up?"

"Yes." He rolled his eyes.

"Ass face." She pointed at him.

"Kim, you do know you're insane don't you?" she just chuckled and looked out the window. The empty dirt road was definitely in need of some improvements. It was bumpy and dusty. She quite liked how this one's surrounding landscape seemed to be more untouched than the others.

"When are we going to stop off for the night? I'm tired." She whined.

"Put your head down now then, we won't be stopping for a while."

Kim tutted loudly and rested her head on the window, looking out again at the blurs passing her by. She heard Nathan's cell phone ringing and then him talking in a hushed tone. Her eyes began to close, the tiredness kicking in when all of a sudden the car came to a halting stop. Before she knew what was going on she was tossed around her seat, whacking her head off of the window whilst Nathan made an abrupt and harsh turn.

She realised he had turned and was beginning to go the wrong way, driving back the way they had come on the other side of the road. Kim was confused and annoyed, she didn't want to have to run away from crazy Japanese men again and hoped there was another explanation for Nathan's crazy actions.

"What the fuck are you doing?"

"Change of plans sweetheart." He spoke but she knew he was distracted. He had already hung up the phone and was flying down the empty road quicker than ever before on this entire trip.

"Change of plans?" Kim furrowed her brows at him, not understanding.

He flashed her a wicked and wide smile before he spoke.

"We're going to Las Vegas Kimmy."

Chapter 12

"Las Vegas? Are you crazy?" Kim asked in bewilderment. "What the hell are we going to do in Las Vegas Nathan?"

"I have something I need to take care of."

"You sound very sketchy... I don't like this plan. I want to go home." She was uneasy about the entire thing regardless of the fact that she had given herself no time to warm to the new change of plans.

"You weren't going home in the first place Kim, we were going to D.C remember?" he scoffed, causing her to narrow her eyes at him in annoyance.

"Yes but at least I thought home might be in the near future. We're literally going back on our steps by days and days just to go to Las Vegas? Couldn't you have decided to go there like-I don't know- when we left Portland? It's going to take us ages." Kim felt as though she was about to have a nervous breakdown.

"Not my problem Sweetheart." He said monotonously.

Normal life was something that was definitely unreachable now, the constant question in her mind was: when would everything go back to the way it was? Tears of wretchedness pricked her eyes, her mind wandered a little more into the topic and then her sadness was replaced with anger.

"We have a punch of crazy Japanese Kung Fu men trying to kill us at any moment and now you're going to drive us all the way back to Las fucking Vegas?!" Her raised voice made Nathan cringe slightly.

"Calm down Kim, god-"

"No, I won't calm down. The quicker you get me to D.C, the quicker I will fully understand what's going on and I'll be safe there too. Why the hell didn't you decide to go to Las Vegas when we were in Portland you dumbass?" she asked the same question he hadn't answered just a moment ago again.

"You're going to be safe, I'm assuring you now."

"Your assurance means jack shit to me. You couldn't care less whether I'm safe or not. Dead or alive, once you get me to D.C, you'll be fine." There was a short silence in the car before Nathan finally spoke. He had been weighing up his options on what to say next and had decided to tell her the truth.

"That was a lie." He admitted, still keeping his eye on the road as they soared past the desolate landscape.

"What?"

"I was lying okay? I told you that to scare you. My boss needs you alive and safe. We're going to Las Vegas and then

I'm taking you to D.C. It's my job to keep you safe and I must admit I'm very good at my job."

"You don't seem to be very good at your job, considering you're prolonging our trip, putting us both in more danger than needed."

"Kim... trust me with this alright?"

"No, not alright. I wouldn't say I could trust you at all actually."

"Well you're just going to have to."

"What's so god damn important in Las Vegas anyway Nathan?" Kim challenged him.

"I'm going to find the people who murdered my parents." Nathan spoke loudly with frustration.

It certainly shut her up. She was completely taken aback. Kim had only learned Nathan's parents were both dead a short time ago but he had never mentioned how they had died and so this caused some surprise after his confession. She was unsure how to act, and didn't know what to do or say.

"It's getting late, maybe we should stop off somewhere soon." Was all Kim could think to say when she opened her mouth. Her voice trailed off as she spoke and she looked away from him, out the window again.

"I want her back here as soon as you can Nathan. I don't care whether you have to drag her by the hair or if she's in a body bag anymore. Once you get her here I don't give a fuck."

The words stung Kim's ears, she had heard every last one loud and clear. Nathan didn't know of her presence nearby yet, he thought she was getting ready for bed. He was sitting out on the balcony of their hotel room with his phone on loudspeaker.

"I understand." He nodded to himself; the change of plan was slightly unsettling for him. First, his boss needed her to be alive and now there was a huge rush to make sure her body physically got to D.C dead or alive. Some things were a little strange and fishy.

"I know you have other things going on at the minute after your discovery. You've been such a good agent over the years and so we can understand completely your need to extend the trip. We just hope you can complete the mission correctly."

"Why are you so keen on Kim being dead or alive now anyways? Didn't you need to question her when I got her to D.C?"

"Things have changed Nathan."

"What has changed? You assigned me this mission for a reason, I should know everything about it. What are you keeping from me?"

"She has something in her arm that we need."

"And what is it exactly that you need?" Kim edged closer to the door, still remaining hidden by the curtains that were pulled over almost all the way.

She wanted to hear this, she needed to hear it. She was scared even more then by the fact that Nathan could kill her at any moment and bring her back to D.C whenever he was done with his business in Las Vegas. It would definitely be the easier option- considering the two were constantly bickering and arguing with each other.

"There's a microchip implanted in her arm holding very important undisclosed details from her father's company. We need it as soon as possible, the information is vital for our case. It's more important than the answers we want from her now."

Kim covered her hand with her mouth, she could have gasped if she had wanted to be more dramatic. She couldn't believe what she was hearing and it made her feel sick. She began to panic and break out in a sweat, but was still frozen in her spot until a breeze came along and blew the curtain hiding her from Nathan.

Nathan's expression sunk, his eyes immediately connecting with hers. The look on her face showed that if she hadn't heard everything, she had certainly heard enough. Kim's heart was racing in her chest and then she finally decided to rip herself from the spot she had been standing in.

She ran quickly in the direction of the door but Nathan, as usual was too quick for her. He told his boss he needed to go and swiftly hung up to run after her. Kim was about to put her hand on the doorknob when Nathan yanked her arm away and pinned her to the wall.

"What do you think you're doing?" he asked. She was surprised at how calm he was acting. His brows were furrowed but his tone was more quizzical than full of fury or rage. Kim hesitated for a minute, tears pricking her eyes again.

"I-I, I'm trying to get out of here. Just let me go Nathan please." She knew she was being silly. She knew he wouldn't allow her to leave but that was all she wanted in that moment.

"Kim you're trying to escape again and you haven't even got any shoes on? Stop being ridiculous."

"No! You don't know what it feels like."

"What what feels like?" Nathan's facial features held an expression of concern as he looked down at her sorrowful face.

"I don't know what's going on around me. Everything is going wrong, my life is a fucking mess and I have no control over when or how that will change. I have no one." He had already let her go to examine her deflated exterior.

Kim had sunk to the ground, her back to the door as she covered her face with her hands. Tears escaped her eyes and she knew she would curse herself later on for coming across as weak in front of Nathan.

"You could just kill me now if you wanted. It would be easier for you. All you need now is this thing in my arm, and that's all the people on my father's side need too."

"I'm guessing you heard everything then?" he asked but she still wouldn't look at him. She wiped away her tears and closed her eyes before nodding yes in reply to his question.

"The night they got into our room one of them was checking my arm. I didn't know it then but it was because they were making sure it was still there, feeling around for it I suppose. If even the CIA doesn't value my life, the rest won't either."

"Kim..." She heard Nathan's voice close to her then and was a little startled when he wrapped his arms around her in a loose embrace. "Shh Kim, stop crying." He urged her gently.

She felt the soft touch of his hands removing hers from her face. He tilted her chin up in order to look at him. He seemed to be more than a little apprehensive and it surprised her.

"No." she said weakly, continuing to let tears pore down her face. He reached out and wiped some away.

"I know you don't trust me, but you're going to be safe with me Kim. I won't let anything happen to you while you're with me. Whether we're in Las Vegas or D.C." Nathan spoke with finality but nothing felt final at all to her. She looked unsure but he only held her tighter in response.

He knew he was getting himself into trouble by even considering the actions he chose to take that night. He understood how feelings were beginning to creep up on him. He could never love someone again- it was too dangerous and Nathan had learned that the hard way. He could never love a girl like Kim, but that didn't mean he couldn't care about her. The last few days they had spent together had made him realise he had no choice in the matter of what he would feel.

Nathan was aware of the fact that Kim didn't believe him and why should she? Everyone else in her life had let her down but he made a promise to himself and Kim then that he would protect her, unlike other people in her life. He would not let her down. Nathan's thoughts were completely and absolutely absurd, but he just had to deal with it.

He stayed with her for a while, the two sitting on the soft carpet in the room until he decided it was time for bed. Kim was exhausted, physically and emotionally, he knew that she needed to sleep. They both got ready and followed the same routine they did every night, ending with Nathan binding their wrists together.

Kim hadn't said much, she barely opened her mouth at all since her eruption a couple of minutes ago. She was too tired to cry anymore, Nathan had surprisingly been a comforting presence she needed that night. A ghost of a small smile fell upon her lips as soon as she felt his hand wrapping around hers in the handcuffs. She didn't want to be happy because of him but she was and there was no stopping that.

His boss's words wrung in his mind again as he felt the softness of her hand wrapped in his. Nathan knew it would be the easier thing to do but that would be a task extremely difficult for him to even contemplate. Nathan cared about Kim, he understood the challenges she had to face and believed her completely by then although a part of him was still apprehensive about it.

He knew for sure he had already grown too attached.

Chapter 13

After that night, Kim refused to break down in front of Nathan again. She was a strong young woman and although crying didn't make a person weak, it certainly made her feel weak. That was the exact opposite of how she wanted to be perceived by him or anyone else for that matter.

Nathan had noticed her cool exterior and how she had been holding back a little in their recent conversations. She hadn't opened up to him again since then, and that had been almost a week ago. He was confused and disappointed, although he would never let it show. He could sense something was off with Kim but remained indifferent in front of her. He reckoned a reason for it was because of the growing tension between the pair of them that neither wanted to talk about.

They were so close to Las Vegas by then. After that night Nathan made sure to get there fast. He limited their breaks, drove until later in the evening and got up earlier to start driving again every morning. As much as Kim wanted to complain about it, she couldn't because she knew he was doing it for her, in order to make her feel safe.

She seemed to be on edge constantly when they were driving and even in the safety of the hotel rooms they shared together. She got little sleep every night and although she had never told Nathan, he knew it was because she was troubled and apprehensive about everything. Kim was living in fear that more people may come to get them but that fear hadn't become a reality just yet. Nathan was the only thing that took her mind off of it,even just a little sometimes.

"I don't want to talk about my friends." Kim said with little emotion behind her words.

She had been staying away from him for the past few days. Well, as far away as she possibly could considering they had to live and sleep in the same bed together. Although keeping physically away from him was difficult, mentally, she was steering clear of most personal conversations until right then, when she could avoid it no more.

They were sitting down to a quick dinner in a small diner they found just off the highway. Both had ordered and Nathan was trying to learn more about Kim's life back in Chicago.

"Why not?" he challenged her, knowing there was something particularly fishy about the way she had refused out straight. Other topics were a little harder for her to turn down. Why would one not want to talk about their friends?

"Because they aren't my friends anymore. There's no point in living in the past."

"So Shane is still your fiancé?" he quirked an eyebrow at her, trying to prove a point but she managed to find a way to worm her way out of the discussion he wanted.

"Why? Are you planning on popping the question to me Nathan? How sweet of you." She couldn't help but joke with him sometimes, she felt like she needed to think it was the wrong thing to do but she couldn't help it. Kim smirked but Nathan stared blankly at her for a moment in return.

"Answer me."

"No. Of course not." She rolled her eyes, knowing exactly what he would say next.

"Well, you said it yourself. Shane isn't your fiancé anymore, so why didn't you mind talking about him?"

"Because I wasn't thinking when I told you about him." Because I lied to you about him, she thought to herself.

"Well why don't you just stop thinking now and tell me about your old friends?"

"You're intolerable sometimes Nathan." She rolled her eyes. The way she spoke left a hint of honesty behind, like she was about to open up and that she did- as much as she felt able. "In the end, none of them would come away with me." Because you didn't want any of them to, her subconscious butted in.

"Why is that?" he quizzed her but she shrugged in reply.

"I told some of them about my father and what happened, I said I had enough and I was moving. They all reacted the same, as sympathetic as ever but not really giving that much of a shit." Sympathetic because they felt sorry for what your pathetic life had become and what your pathetic fiancé had done... she couldn't stop her thoughts.

"You can't really expect people to just jump up and leave with you Kim, regardless of whether they were your friends or not."

"They owed me." Kim tried to hide the anger erupting inside of her but it was a challenging task to do. He sense her discomfort but couldn't help but ask one last question.

"For what?"

"They lied to me, like everyone else." She had said too much, she was aware of that. And so when he opened his mouth to speak she jumped up from the booth they were sitting at and spoke again. "I need to find the bathroom." Her tone was dark and full of emotion. It made him feel terrible then.

"Kim-"

"Forget it." She cut across him and went on her way.

Tears pricked her eyes as she walked with her head down into the bathrooms. It wasn't until she was inside the safety of a cubicle, alone, that she allowed herself to burst into disconsolate tears. She didn't want to think about Shane Parker, she didn't want to think about her friends and she definitely didn't want to think about the betrayal from both sides that fell down on her like a tonne of bricks when her life had already spiralled out of control.

Everything was a train wreck, one that she wanted to give up on completely in that moment but she reminded herself that she was strong, she was tough and she could also get through all of this. Despite being aware of the fact that ignoring everything that had happened five years ago wouldn't help her at all, she still wanted to try and do so.

She wiped away her tears after a couple of minutes of crying and splashed water in her face once she exited the cubicle. Kim looked at her reflection in the mirror and tried to give herself a pep talk. She was ready to go back outside and face Nathan.

He was relieved to see her smiling face reappearing at the table in front of him but then noticed it was plastered on with great effort. A part of Nathan ached for her. She had been through a lot, so had he but their lives turned into disasters for very different reasons.

For Nathan could not control the death of his parents, it was something that had just happened and he had some family members to help him after all of that had happened to him at the young age of sixteen. Death, in his parents' case was not a choice, but the betrayal of Kim's family and friends was something they all had control over and chose to do so regardless of how Kim would feel afterward.

Her own father had decided to lie to her, her fiancé decided to betray her by working with her father and her friends- he didn't quite know what they had done but understood it was something that Kim would never forget. Nathan's parents loved him, and if given the choice would not have left him to live a very lonely life, sorrow following him around for what felt like forever.

Kim never told him about what happened between Shane and her friends that day. She just couldn't. And she was also glad that he hadn't asked about it again. Instead, he reached his hand across the table and took hers. He rubbed his thumb over her soft skin, an attempt to comfort her. But his touch was too much for her to handle. Such a small gesture had left tingles on the areas he had touched. Nathan could sense it too, but she was the first to pull away.

There was tension for the rest of the day in the car. Being in such a small place for such a long time made it unbearable for Kim. The fact that she knew Nathan wouldn't try anything with her was killing her. She knew it would be difficult to get him to give in, a lot more difficult than it would be for her if the roles were reversed. Kim wanted something to get her mind off of everything and a night with Nathan seemed like the perfect idea.

His gaze flickered from the road ahead to her multiple times in the car. The guilt from the pain he had caused her earlier over dinner had made him agree to play eye spy. Her face lit up when he said yes. They played until Nathan decided to call it a night and found a hotel room.

Kim's heart began racing once he opened the door to their room and threw the duffle bag on the bed. They had cleaned their clothes a few days ago so Kim fished around to find her pyjamas, she could feel Nathan's eyes on her for the entire time. She had her back to him, trying to stay as far away from him as she possibly could in a small hotel room.

"I need to shave." He mumbled to himself before he too began looking in the duffle bag and finding the things he needed.

"Hurry up." Kim rolled her eyes as he entered the bathroom. "I need to shower soon."

"I know you do." He replied, she could hear him from the other side of the closed door.

"Dumbass!" she called back.

He chuckled loudly and took a very long time in the bathroom. He decided to have a shower and shave. Nathan was met with Kim's face up close to him as soon as he opened the door. She had been waiting outside for a very long time waiting for him to be finished.

"Well you took your sweet time didn't you?" she said in a vexed tone, remaining in her spot.

Kim knew Nathan wouldn't give in to her, but she thought trying would be fun. She enjoyed seeing him frustrated.

"Kim..." he warned, their lips just inches away from each other.

"What?" Kim acted innocent, her eyes lingering on his lips.

"Get out of the way."

"Why?" she leaned a little closer, a giggle escaping her lips. He knew exactly what she was doing, but it took him some time to move away and stop himself.

"Move." He grumbled before pushing past her. Kim was the one laughing then; she took her clothes and headed in for a relaxing shower.

As soon as she got out, she dried herself off and got into just her underwear before exiting the bathroom. Kim pretended to fish around in the duffle bag for something when she opened the bathroom door and stepped into the room again. Nathan's breath hitched in his throat at the sight of her, he was sitting on the couch facing her and could see every part of her on display, head to toe.

"Kim..." Nathan spoke again that same cautious tone, but who was he warning? Kim or himself?

She turned her head and waited for a reply, still acting as innocent as ever.

"Stop."

"Stop what?" she asked, rather smugly.

"Put some clothes on."

"It's too warm, I'm going to just skip wearing clothes tonight."

"God damn it Kim." Nathan muttered under his breath before standing up and walking towards her and the bag.

"You're such a stick in the mud."

"Because I don't want us doing something we'll both regret."

"I won't regret it." She stated truthfully. Nathan on the other hand, knew it he would regret it.

Although a part of him was telling him no, another was telling him yes. He wanted Kim there and then, more so than all of the other days or nights they had spent together and she wanted him too so what was the problem? She had clearly stated it was just sex, he knew that was all he could deal with too but it was good to know they would be on the same page.

Kim had this pull towards her, swallowing him up. She was powerful, her mind and body, Nathan felt as though he was at war with himself for a couple of minutes while he stood in front of her. She looked intensely at him, trying to figure him out. She took a step closer and brought her hand up to his chin. Her fingers ran softly over his jaw line and then she leaned in to place light kisses around his mouth.

Nathan closed his eyes for a moment, unable to take it all. Her touch was like fire, he craved more and more of her. His hand went to tangle in her hair as he pulled her closer to his lips for a passionate kiss. Kim took his hands and placed them on her bare waist. He felt her soft skin and moved closer to ravish her mouth again, this time with a kiss full of lust and complete want.

But then Nathan pulled away and looked at her. He shouldn't do this, he couldn't do this, but he wanted to.

"Put something on and go to bed." His voice was husky and low. She looked up at him before speaking.

"Or else?" she daringly said.

"Or else I won't be able to stop myself." There was a short silence until she spoke again, neither had pulled away yet.

"Then don't." she whispered. Her words stirred something within him, they gave him the ability to let go. And so within a matter of seconds, he had picked her up and began to kiss her senseless. Kim was getting what she wanted, and what she knew he wanted too. It was a win win situation, or so she thought.

Nathan was everything she had been expecting and more. She did not regret anything she done that night which wasn't a surprise. He was enjoying a cigarette and held her close in his arms afterward, wondering why it felt so nice to have her so near. Nathan couldn't think straight, he felt strange because what he was thinking was unexpected. He could not find an ounce of regret in his body for what they had both done together. Instead, he wanted more.

Nathan fell asleep first, his arms wrapped tightly around her. Once he finished his cigarette he settled down and drifted off quickly. As soon as she knew he was asleep she shrugged out of his firm grip and slept on her own side of the bed with her back to him.

Men were assholes, she reminded herself, even Nathan. Kim didn't need to over think anything in that moment. She just needed to remember despite how sincere and caring he had been towards her over the past couple of days, she couldn't grow to like him in any way. Instead of being used, she would be the user.

Chapter 14

"Kim, we're in a public place now. Let's not get too ahead of ourselves..." Nathan spoke into their kiss.

"Okay." Kim had moved only a centimetre away so that when she spoke, her lips brushed off of his.

In the week that had passed since their first night together, neither were able to stay away from each other. What they had between them was definitely just a physical thing, both understood that completely. Kim had stayed true to her word and was close to him physically but emotionally, she was distant.

Kim had always steered the conversation elsewhere when Nathan brought up things from her past. She felt like she had shared enough with him, maybe even a little too much and now she wanted to refrain from telling him any more. Nathan had noticed this straight away and had managed to not say anything about it, yet. But it had been on the tip of his tongue for a while. He found himself wanting to know more about her. She was an interesting character, a book that was snapped shut every time he went to inspect the pages.

Kim was sitting on a washing machine in a quiet launderette they had stopped at to wash all of their clothes again. Nathan was between her legs, his body close to hers, and his hands were around her waist. He examined her smiling face for a moment as she wrapped her hands around his neck. He then went in for another kiss, this time biting her lip a little at the end.

"I thought we weren't getting too ahead of ourselves?" she raised an eyebrow at him and laughed a little.

"Oh yes, I forgot..." he chuckled at her.

She saw that the clothes in the dryer behind him were finished and so pushed him a little in order to get herself down off of the machine.

"We have things to do Nathan, we can't be standing around all day doing nothing." She said playfully while rolling her eyes.

"We weren't exactly doing nothing." She could sense he was close behind her as she sorted out there clothes.

"Come and help me." Kim muttered, her mind beginning to wander into deadly territory.

She wondered whether she had made the right decision after that night. It seemed as though she was getting too close to Nathan too quickly and she didn't like that side of it, but everything else felt right. Her doubts were easily forgotten with his company but she was unsure whether that was a good or bad thing? Kim hadn't decided yet.

The two packed their things back into the duffle bag together and left the launderette. Kim was overjoyed when Nathan had told her they would reach Las Vegas in a matter of a few short hours. But after her happiness had subsided, she wondered how hard it would be for her when they were back on their way to D.C again.

"Kim." Nathan eyed her curiously while focusing on driving also. She was being particularly quiet that day and he wanted to know why.

"Hmm?" she asked, not turning her head away from the window to even look at him.

"Are you alright?" he placed his hand on her thigh, the contact causing her to finally catch eyes with him.

"I'm fine." Kim nodded, although not really convincing Nathan the slightest bit.

"Why are you being so quiet?" he was genuinely concerned.

"I'm just- thinking. That's all." He took his hand away and put it back on the steering wheel.

"You can talk to me if you want Kim."

"All you want to talk about is Chicago." Kim didn't get angry; she didn't raise her voice or sound in any way hostile.

"Well, that's because I'm interested in your life back in Chicago."

"Interested in how shitty everyone was to me back there?" she scoffed. "That's great." She said sarcastically.

"No, it's not like that. I just think learning about your past shows me what's made you be the person you are right now."

"Wow you're getting deep today aren't you?" Kim tried to joke.

"Why can't we have a serious conversation sometimes?"

"Because they're always about me and all of the pain I've had to go through. All of the terrible things I've had to endure and shitty people I've had to meet. It's never once about you." She had a point but Nathan didn't want to agree with her.

"Kim..."

"What? You wanted a serious conversation so here it is? Why can you just randomly ask me questions about sensitive topics whenever you god damn feel like it but I can never talk about your past and what's happened to you?"

"Because my past is a difficult topic-"

"And mine is too. I'm sorry I don't want to talk about my terrible fiancé or my sly friends or my deceiving father. They aren't difficult things to talk about..." Kim spoke sarcastically.

There was a pause in the car for a minute or two, Nathan was figuring out what to say next while she turned to look out the window again. He was thinking, wondering why he felt less uncomfortable to talk to her about his parents or his childhood than he usually did around others. He had never once let a woman in and also didn't plan to do so either but Kim... she was different and that shook him up a little. In such a short time, he had discovered so many sides to her personality. He had found out her weaknesses, her joys and what made her laugh.

Nathan had come to a realisation that she was a broken girl who had run away from her troubled past, but this didn't make him want to be as far away from her as possible, it only made him feel less alone. Because he too, was broken, he too had a grim past that could not ever be fixed completely. Sometimes being broken wasn't a bad thing, that was something difficult for most to comprehend but Nathan, he understood entirely. More than Kim would ever know.

Yes, they had spent only a couple of weeks together, but in that time Nathan had made a connection with her that he was afraid of telling her about.

"Want to play a game?" he asked, not giving up yet.

"I'm not in the mood for eye spy. The one fucking time you'll agree to play with me is the worst time possible."

"I never mentioned eye spy Sweetheart."

"What then?" she looked at him then.

"Twenty questions."

"No." Kim said straight away.

"Why not?"

"The same reason I don't want to have a serious conversation with you." His words made him scoff a little.

"We both get twenty questions." This definitely caught her attention, Nathan could physically see the interesting look falling upon her face in a matter of seconds. It made him smile.

"Okay then, you go first."

"What happened to your mom?" he asked. He knew she wasn't dead, it just seemed like she was never really talked about like her father was. Kim thought for a moment before speaking.

"She lives back in Chicago with my father and brothers. She stayed out of the whole feud my father and I had going on before I left. Makes her as bad as the rest in my opinion." She spoke with a straight and truthful tone.

"Oh."

"Have you ever been in a serious relationship with anyone?" Kim had thought about the order her questions were going to go in, her more difficult ones were saved for the middle of the game.

"No."

"No? That's all I get?" he rolled his eyes when she spoke but continued on.

"I can't really say much. I've never been with a girl for more than a couple weeks, nothing has ever been serious." he blatantly lied.

"So you've never been in love?" she asked, coming across a little too eager then.

"Don't waste your questions Kim... Besides- it's my turn." he wanted to get off the topic as quick as possible. Nathan didn't want to think about it anymore.

"Did you get along with your brothers?"

"No. Not that much really. They wanted to be thoroughly involved in the company and got jealous of me sometimes because of how close my father kept me in decision making. Do you have other family you're close to, or friends?"

"Yes, I'm close to my Aunt and Uncle who I lived with when I was sixteen. I have friends too you know, I'm not a loner. Why are you asking, are you looking for a date of some sort from one of them?" he teased.

"Don't waste your questions Nathan." She mimicked him before smiling smugly.

"Did you love Shane?" Kim was surprised by his third question being about her fiancé, she at least thought he would have eased into the topic a little gentler.

"Of course I loved Shane. I would never have agreed to marry him if I didn't." She was quick to answer. The honesty in her words made Nathan feel a little jealous although he knew he was being utterly ridiculous.

"Do you still love him?" she was even more taken aback by the fourth question and stopped to think.

"Are we asking questions in twos now instead of taking turns?"

"Answer me Kim." Nathan's tone was almost cold.

He wanted to know the answer to his question because he could think of no other reason for Kim's constant refusal to talk about him other than the one time they stopped in the car. It was a logical answer, why would anyone want to talk about someone they couldn't have but still wanted. If she loved Shane, she would hate to love him but sometimes people don't get a say in who they love, their heart decides instead.

"No."

"That's all you're going to say?" she had forced him to say more in his answer and now she had to follow her own rules.

"I guess I'm just not fully over what he done to me, that doesn't mean I'm still in love with him. I couldn't love him anymore. I fell in love with a different Shane, not the one that he became in our relationship." Kim had said too much, she always said too much around Nathan.

"So if he became the person he used to be, would you love him again?" This time, Kim turned to look at Nathan's face completely. She couldn't understand what his fixation was with her and Shane's relationship.

"No. I don't forgive easily Nathan. So just remember that before you go pulling shit on me while we're on this trip. I am the most unforgiving person you will ever meet."

Nathan felt like he should be convinced, but he wasn't. It shouldn't matter to him whether Kim was still in love with Shane or not, but for some reason it did and it felt strange.

"I've gathered that already." He replied.

"How old were you when you lost your virginity?" Nathan scoffed at her question. "You never said twenty questions had to be serious..." she added.

"Fifteen."

"How-"

"No Nathan, it's still my turn. You asked three in a row now shut up and let me speak." She ordered him, causing his lips to turn upward in a wide smile.

"You're crazy." He muttered lowly to himself.

"What do you do when you're not working?"

"I work some more." Kim had to roll her eyes at his statement.

"That's so boring. I hate a man that's too dedicated to his job."

"It's a good thing we're not together then isn't it?"

"I'm too good for you, that's why we're not together." She said light-heartedly. "And because you're on a mission to bring me to D.C and never have to see me again after that."

"I'm clearly the one that would be too good for you." He laughed at her statement.

"Whatever. I'm cold, can you turn down the AC?"

"No, I'm warm. Here," he reached in with one hand to the back seat and threw her a blanket. "Take this."

"Oh, how nice? Do you keep your blankets in the back seat next to your spare guns and cable ties?" Nathan couldn't help but chortle loudly at Kim's sarcasm.

"Yes I do, that's your fifth question ruined. Now it's my turn to ask."

"No, that's not fair!"

"It is. Now, when was the last time you've ever been with a man before this trip?" Nathan was curious, and thought it may take her a long time to think about the answer but instead, she answered almost straight away.

"A couple of days before I bumped into you. And what about you?"

"I've never been with a man Kim, another question ruined." He laughed.

"You're so unfair."

"If you could take back what you did to your father and running away, would you do it?" It took Kim a long time to answer this one.

"I'm not sure anymore..." she mumbled but Nathan could still hear what she had said. Her lack of confidence when answering made him frown. "Nathan?"

"Yes?"

"I want to ask you a question, but you don't have to answer it if you don't want to." She warned him.

"Go on."

"What happened to your parents?" Nathan didn't speak a word for a minute or two, all he did was let out a few long breaths before gulping.

"They were both shot off duty one day when they were on the way to pick me up from football practice. They were murdered and I want to get revenge."

"I'm sure you will. You seem like a determined person." His icy tone scared her a little but she didn't tell him that. He nodded at her in reply and then asked another question.

"What did your friends back in Chicago do to you? Why aren't they your friends anymore?"

"I told you already." She said as she wrapped the blanket around herself and got comfortable.

"I know there's more to the story. Tell me the truth."

"I found out that they were keeping a lot of secrets from me. Not just your typical white lies, things that were a lot more serious than that."

"You're turn."

"I'm getting kind of tired." She said before yawning as if on que. "We can continue this later. You've had eight questions, I've had seven."

"But it was beginning to get interesting?"

"It really wasn't..." she laughed a little. "Wake me up when we get there." Kim turned then and rested her head on the window before closing her eyes and drifting off to sleep.

Chapter 15

"Wake up." Nathan spoke gently while shaking her a little. "We're here Kim."

"Hmm?" she asked, one eye still closed. She could see they were in a parking lot and blinked a couple of times then to clear the sleep from her eyes.

"Let's go." He laughed at her before getting out of the car and shutting his door.

Kim did as she was told and met him at the front of the car. He was holding the duffle bag and with his spare arm, held it out for her to link. She took his arm and they both walked through the car park to the main entrance of the extravagant looking hotel.

She looked in awe at the sight of the bright lights amongst the dark sky and the huge buildings towering over her. As soon as they got inside, Kim couldn't help but feel self-conscious by what she was wearing and how she looked. The hotel was beautifuly decorated and only people dressed in the best of clothes could be spotted.

Nathan noticed how she held onto his arm a little tighter then as they reached the front desk.

"I have a reservation under the name Smith." He spoke with great confidence.

"Just give me a minute sir." The receptionist scanned through the information on her computer before organising the room with him. She handed him two key cards at the end of the conversation and told them what floor they were on.

Kim couldn't stop her eyes from wandering everywhere around this new, extravagant place. Of course, back in Chicago, she would stay in fancy places like this and associate with important people. All of this clearly displayed money, power and status that reeked off of the place and people here would not have been out of the ordinary for her or her family. But it had been five years since she left that life behind and things were different now.

"Holy shit." Kim exclaimed once they entered their 'room'. Nathan had forgotten to tell her he had booked a deluxe suite for seven nights there. "This place is huge." She spoke in astonishment.

"I know." He said, setting the duffle bag aside. His eyes followed her as she ran to the huge bed and jumped on it. Nathan couldn't help but chuckle at the sight of her and walked to the edge of the bed. "Enjoying yourself?"

"Yes." She said as she snuggled up to the endless pillows and cushions laid out of the bed. Her eyes were closed and she felt as though she might fall asleep any minute.

"Don't get too comfortable, we're going out."

"What? Why?"

"We have people to see, things to do."

"But it's almost ten?" Nathan scoffed at her excuse.

"The party's only starting now, this is Las Vegas Kim. Everything keeps going all night."

"Where do we have to go? Can't I just stay here?" she groaned.

"We're going to meet my friend." He noticed how she perked up a little once he said that.

"Who is it?"

"You'll just have to wait and see..."

"C'mon? What if I use one of my questions?"

"Fine then." He rolled his eyes and crossed his arms. Kim sat up before she spoke.

"Who are we going to meet?"

"His name's Stephen. He's a close friend of mine since we were both young and he's going to help me out with my plans." Kim only nodded and got up from the bed.

"Where are we going to meet him?" She was very curious about his friend Stephen. She wondered whether he too worked in the CIA or not.

"We're going out for a quick bite to eat." Kim looked down at her clothing and hoped they weren't going anywhere fancy. She had nothing at all to wear. "Don't worry, we're both going shopping tomorrow. I need you dressed to impress for the week ahead of us Sweetheart."

"What have you got planned?"

"You'll see." She gulped at his answer. She felt more than anxious at the fact that he was withholding his motives but couldn't say much else; Nathan had already grabbed his keys and was headed towards the door.

It took them around fifteen minutes to get to a small diner that was away from all of the hustle and bustle of casinos and high-rise buildings. Once they entered, Kim spotted a man sitting at a table alone. Nathan smiled instantly when he saw the man and began walking towards him, not saying a word to Kim.

"Nathan." The man spoke warmly to him and shook his hand.

"Good to see you Stephen."

"Good to see you too, but even better to see this little beauty. And what might your name be?" Stephen spoke flirtatiously. Kim opened her mouth to speak but Nathan had already won the race she was not aware of.

"This is Kim." There was darkness hidden within Nathan's tone that made her eye him with interest. He put an arm around her as he spoke and held her close to the side of his body almost possessively.

"Jeez Nathan, relax." Stephen rolled his eyes but sat down then at their booth. "I'm just saying hi." He chuckled. Nathan knew he was being a little ridiculous but wouldn't admit it. He only gestured for Kim to sit into the booth before him and then followed her.

"Don't mind him Stephen. He can act like a caveman sometimes." She rolled her eyes back at Nathan's friend and the two laughed while Nathan narrowed his eyes at the two of them.

"So how have you been man?" Stephen finally asked once they had ordered.

"Pretty stressed out. I'm just happy to finally have gotten this far, the job's almost done but that doesn't mean I can relax yet. I won't be happy until it's over."

Kim wanted to ask what he was talking about but felt like staying quiet for most of the time they all shared together. She listened intently to the two men's conversation, trying to take in everything she possibly could. She was growing tired then and wanted to go back to the hotel to catch some sleep. Kim yawned and wrapped both her small arms around Nathan's big one, leaning her head on his upper arm. He continued on talking but not before moving his hand to sit on her thigh underneath the table.

"We better go soon." Nathan sighed. "I'll talk to you tomorrow alright?" he spoke to Stephen.

"Cool. I look forward to seeing you again Kim." Stephen winked at her, earning a glare from Nathan. "I'm joking Nathan, I know the Bro Code."

"I should hope so."

"Goodnight Stephen." Kim smiled politely at him, knowing he was just playing with Nathan. She didn't get a creepy, pervy vibe from him yet so understood his flirtatious actions were in fact a joke.

"I'll see you tomorrow." Nathan nodded at Stephen before taking Kim's hand and heading outside to this car.

The drive was quiet and there was tension building up that Kim couldn't ignore. They arrived at the hotel and once inside their suite, Nathan shut the door quite loudly. She turned around to see an extremely pissed off looking Nathan undoing his tie. By then, all exhaustion had left Kim, and she had become curious.

She let out a sigh before walking into the living room to sit herself down. Nathan strided into the bathroom and shut the door behind him. He took a deep breath and looked at himself in the mirror. He wondered where this rage had come from?

Nathan knew Stephen for a very long time, he trusted him completely, which was very uncommon for a man like Nathan. But all of a sudden he felt the need to be protective over her even though the two had nothing much between them. He was left not really knowing what to do or how to act.

As soon as Kim heard the bathroom door opening up again, she opened her eyes. She was lying on one of the sofas, waiting for him to come closer. Her eyes followed him like a hawk when she noticed he was nearing her but stopped at the armchair, remaining on his feet.

"Aren't you going to sit down?" she questioned.

"No." he grumbled.

"Nathan..." he looked into her eyes then and blinked a couple of times, taking in the beautiful sight of her relaxed figure lounging across the couch.

"What?"

"I'm using one of my questions which means you have to answer me. What has you so worked up?"

"You know what Kim."

"Stephen? He barely said three words to me, why are you so bothered by it? Isn't he a good friend of yours?"

"I-I don't know." She had a good point, Nathan knew it.

"Well then, sit your ass down and stop sulking." As much as he didn't like her telling him what to do, he listened to her anyway and sat down on the same couch as her, moving her legs onto his lap. Kim switched on the TV and flicked through the stations until she found something to watch.

The two sat there in a comfortable silence until Kim drifted off to sleep. It was two in the morning when Nathan decided to wake her up but she wouldn't budge.

"Just leave me here please." She grumbled, her eyes still closed.

"God Kim, you haven't stopped sleeping all day. Get your lazy ass up and get to bed."

"No." she groaned and turned around on the sofa.

"Fine then." He said. She thought she had won the fight and so smiled to herself as she got comfortable but then she felt his arms wrap around her and pick her up. Too tired to even put up a fight, she said nothing until he placed her down on their bed.

"Thank you." Kim smiled again and closed her eyes, snuggling up in the sheets.

"Whatever." He said and got into bed beside her. Kim was half asleep again by then, but felt him near her.

"Goodnight Nathan." She said sweetly to him. It made him smile to himself.

"Goodnight." He spoke and turned in the bed. He wasn't expecting what she did next.

Kim moved closer to him under the covers so that she could rest her head on his chest. Instantly, his response was the wrap his arm around her and then pull her closer. He heard her light breathing and felt how she draped her arm over his body.

Nathan couldn't help but come to the realisation that her touch felt right. Kim lying in his arms felt like the realest thing he had ever experienced, she was what he wanted and needed right then. As those thoughts processed in his mind, he felt the urge to remind himself that they were the worst things he could feel in that moment. It felt like the onset of a relationship that didn't exist and that was the truth, they were not together, they never would be.

"Goodnight Kim." He said after kissing her forehead gently. He looked down at her plump lips and her closed eyes and tried his best to ignore the panic shooting through him. Kim chuckled breathlessly then whispered.

"You already said that."

"Shut up and go to sleep already." He laughed too and held her tighter then before the two drifted off to sleep.

"No, I don't want to get up yet." Kim groaned and turned on her side in bed to face him.

"We have to do things today, c'mon." he rolled his eyes at her laziness but lay in bed next to her still.

"Can't I have ten more minutes?" she batted her eyes at him and spoke sweetly. Nathan had a stern look on his face, showing little emotion.

"No." he spoke monotonously.

"But this bed is so much more comfortable than all of the other ones we've had...and you know how much I love sleeping."

"Kim..." he warned her. He wanted to give in, he was so close but he refrained from opening his mouth again.

Nathan watched her carefully as she traced patterns on his arm, her eyes moved to his, a certain look in them that he knew was familiar. Kim moved to straddle his waist and leaned down to kiss his neck. She felt his hands move to hold her hips as her lips moved to his jawline and closer to his mouth.

"You also know how much I love when you-"

"Kim. Go and get ready." He cut her off before she could say any more, knowing exactly what she was trying to do. They both had a busy day and night ahead of them. They had little time to waste.

"Oh fine then." Kim had given up and got up out of bed. "Where are we going?" she asked as she made her way to the bathroom.

"Shopping." He turned to look at the bathroom door once he noticed she had stuck her head back out.

"You'd rather go shopping than get laid Nathan? Some-times I wonder..." she sighed before sticking her head back inside the bathroom. Nathan snickered loudly and heard the shower turning on.

"I'm not sure whether I should feel insulted or not!" she called out to him to which he replied with another laugh. She left the bathroom door wide open, hoping he might join her but was more than a little disappointed when he didn't. He was aware of her actions but had to use all of his self-restraint to stop himself from going inside.

He gave her a couple of minutes before he moved from the bed. Once he heard the water stop running, he walked towards the opened bathroom door to find her dancing around in a towel on the polished marble floors. Kim had yet to discover his presence or his eyes watching her attentively. Her grace and elegance came shining through as she done a couple of pirouettes. Kim opened her eyes and jumped once she saw his head peeking through the door frame into the bathroom.

"I was hoping that towel would fall and you wouldn't realise I was here for a couple more minutes." Kim rolled her eyes in response before heading out of the bathroom, holding her towel securely to her body.

"How about you follow your own advice and get ready too?" She couldn't help but feel slightly foolish because of Nathan finding her dancing in the bathroom. But she had an urge to dance and hadn't done so in what felt like so long.

"Okay, okay... Give me ten minutes."

Chapter 16

"You're not wearing that."

"But Nathan... Why not?" Kim almost whined as she looked at him through the mirror facing her.

They were currently out shopping for suitable clothes for both Kim and Nathan. It had been easier to find things for himself, but now was proving to be difficult to find things that he thought were appropriate for Kim to wear. She had already tried on five dresses but he found something wrong with each one of them.

"Because it doesn't suit you."

"But it's red. Red's my favourite colour. Red is sexy."

"Another reason why I don't like it." She had to roll her eyes at his statement then.

"You're being ridiculous Nathan. At this stage we're never going to find something for me to wear on Friday night."

"Why don't I go and pick something out for you?"

"If you bring back something frumpy and grandma-ish, I'm not putting it anywhere near me." She crossed her arms.

"I won't." he nodded at her before going off out into the shop again.

There was no denying that Nathan was being more than a little overprotective of Kim. He already felt jealous of others looking at her body in any of the dresses she tried on so far but he didn't want his emotions to show. Nathan flicked through the racks of dresses and found two that he thought were the best possible options without Kim thinking they covered too much.

"That one looks good on you."

"It's navy. I don't like navy."

"Well... why not try on the other one then."

"I'll be right back." She entered the dressing room again and came out with the black floor-length gown he had picked out. They would both be attending an event with Stephen on Friday night that would be very important and crucial for his plans. Nathan's breath hitched in his throat for just a second at the sight of her. But then again, that had happened each time she came out of the room with a dress on.

"I'm not sure." He found himself saying, although he knew he shouldn't have.

"You're never going to be happy." She said, a little distract-edly as she looked in the mirror at herself at all different angles. The dress was okay, better than the last one he had brought for her. She decided this was the best she was going to get with Nathan.

"Just get that one, it looks good." He said with finality.

"Really? Are you sure it doesn't show off too much of my neck?" she asked, sarcasm dripping from her tone. He narrowed his eyes at her and then spoke again.

"Do you want me to buy you the navy one instead?"

"No." Kim replied straight away.

"Then shut up."

"You shut up."

"No you shut up."

"No you." Nathan decided to let her have the last word this time.

They shopped around for more outfits for Kim and then headed back to their hotel room to get ready for the night they had ahead of them. Once dressed smartly in the new things they had bought, they went downstairs to meet Stephen in the lobby of the hotel before going out to dinner.

Again, Kim listened carefully to everything both men were saying and felt like she was being kept in the dark about a lot of things. She was interested; she wanted to know Nathan's plans and also didn't want to sit there not opening her mouth all night. But something was holding her back, she wasn't quite sure how to act with Stephen around since Nathan had been so hot-headed the last time. Then, further into the night, Kim could care less about Nathan's reaction later on when she heard her name being mentioned.

"So where does Kim come into all of this?" She instantly perked up at the sound of her name leaving Stephen's lips. Her eyes flickered from one man to the other when she spotted Nathan giving Stephen a dark and intense look.

"Nowhere."

"But you said-"

"She's not part of the plan anymore."

"So I was before?" she asked, earning a glance from both Nathan and Stephen. Nathan felt slightly caught off guard and was unable to say anything for a minute.

"No. Stephen doesn't know what he's talking about."

"Yes she was, don't try to make me look like an idiot." Kim could see the quiet rage within Nathan's eyes then, but he took another moment to take a deep breath and calm himself down.

"Initially, yes. But not anymore."

"Why?" She didn't understand why he had lied and not mentioned anything to her.

"Because we were going to use you to honey pot Kevin Green."

"Who's that?" Stephen scoffed at how oblivious she was.

"The person Nathan came here for."

"Stephen..." Nathan warned.

"She needs to know your plan. Who else are you going to use to slip something into Kevin's drink while he isn't looking?"

"Stephen that's enough. You're here to help me not to spill all of my secrets."

"Well I'm just annoyed that we aren't sticking to the original plan and the fact that you haven't figured something out by now."

"Nathan?" Kim called his name quietly, she tugged at the sleeve of his shirt then, forcing him to look at her whilst in the middle of his disagreement.

Kim felt betrayed, but thought she should have known better. The only reason Nathan hadn't killed her yet was because he needed to use her in his plans to find the people who murdered his parents, which could only make them dangerous. She figured her life was probably on the line if she did whatever it was Nathan wanted her to do.

"Kim we can talk about this later." He brushed her off, still angry at Stephen.

"Why don't you want her to do the job?"

"Because she isn't needed for that anymore." He spoke quickly.

"So what exactly is she needed for now? To be your toy? What's suddenly made you change your mind Nathan?" Stephen challenged his friend.

"Kevin Green is a very dangerous man. If Kim was to poison him and she was found out, that would put her in jeopardy and that's something I don't want. I'll figure something out by Friday; just let me deal with it. My decision is final."

Stephen had then decided to talk about something else. Kim was still trying to figure him out, and why he had called his friend out on his lies in front of her, a girl he knew barely anything about. A while after their meal had ended, they decided to part ways. The car ride was quiet the whole time, a tension was almost visible in the small space they were sharing.

Kim didn't know what to say. She couldn't expect anything else from Nathan that to bring her here in order to use her for his own good. It wasn't like they were anything to each other, and so the feeling of betrayal Kim felt was ridiculous in even her own eyes. But she could not help how she felt and that was the problem.

Nathan knew she was processing the conversation she heard over dinner, she appeared to be getting more upset by the minute. He knew she was going to over analyse all of the information she gathered.

All of the previous events were running through her head since that day in the car when Nathan announced they were going to Las Vegas. Was the fact that she would have to do something important for him the only reason he gave in to her? She had no reason to think otherwise.

As soon as they entered their suite, Kim walked briskly into the bathroom. The sound of the door slamming made Nathan flinch and then sigh. He walked towards the door and knocked gently. Nathan waited patiently for her to answer but after a minute or two of silence he knocked once again, louder this time.

"Kim, come out here please."

"No." she called back, her tone was troublous.

"Kim, just let me explain."

"No. Fuck off." He knew she was quite annoyed, and he needed to give her time to calm down but all he wanted was to give her an explanation. Or else her mind would wander and she would make mindless assumptions.

"Kim you're being silly now—"

"No I'm not! God you're such a dick."

"Open the door before I kick it down." His voice was calm and collected. She decided it was better not to answer him. She didn't want to talk to him right then because she was more than a little angry at him. "I decided to make you a part of the plan when I was assigned this mission. There was a possibility that Kevin Green would be in Las Vegas while we were on our trip to D.C so I thought it would be a great opportunity."

"Good for you."

"But once we were actually on the way here, I changed my mind. You heard what I said back at the restaurant Kim. It would be too risky."

"Bullshit Nathan!" Kim stormed towards the door, unlocked it and threw it open. She was surprised when she saw he was so close but stood right in front of him, staring at him angrily. "You were trying to butter me up all this time so that I would honey pot some random guy for you. Don't take me for a fool."

"I knew you would think that." He pinched the bridge of his nose as he spoke.

"Because it's the truth." She shot back in a rage.

"No it's not."

"And you know what I find very fucking funny about all of this? You would've gladly let me to seduce some man once you were benefiting from it but I'm not allowed to wear a red fucking dress?"

"Kim, it's just a dress."

"Well red's my favourite colour!" there was a silence for a minute until she spoke again. "That's not even the point. The point is you had sex with me so I would do something in return for you."

"Can you even hear yourself right now? You're being ridiculous. If that was my plan all along why would I change it?"

"Maybe you grew a conscience. I don't know?" she shrugged.

"You have to trust me Kim-"

"I don't have to do anything. I've been screwed over too many times in my life to listen to another asshole like you talk to me about trust." Tears pricked her eyes as she spoke and all he wanted to do then was take her in his arms and hold her.

"Please just- please believe me Kim." He took the step between them and wiped away her tears with his thumbs, holding her face then. "I changed my mind once we were on the way to D.C. It's too dangerous now and I don't want to risk anything."

"Why didn't you want to tell me? Back there in the restaurant you started to pretend like Stephen wasn't telling the truth."

"I don't know, I guess I didn't want you to find out. I knew you would take it the wrong way."

He began to caress her cheek. Nathan looked at her beautiful face, her features filled with sorrow and an unsureness he detected clearly. She could not look at him, her mind and heart going in different directions. She wanted to believe Nathan, but after a past full of betrayal and pain, trusting someone was a difficult thing for Kim to do.

"Look at me Kim." He urged her gently, his voice just above a whisper. He tilted her head up a little so she could make eye contact with him but she only shrugged away from him and went to find something to wear to bed.

Kim could feel Nathan's eyes on her as she walked around the room. She went around to her side of the bed and stripped down in front of him, quickly getting changed. He gulped at the sight of her and felt tightness in his chest at the thought that she was upset because of him. Kim felt conflicted and torn in two.

She wanted to yell and get angry at him for lying to her, but the rational side told her that would be wrong. They were nothing to each other, only acquaintances that slept together a couple of times. Although it was cliché, Kim felt this pull towards Nathan, a connection that she never talked about with him. She was too afraid to face what she was feeling and although she was sure it wasn't love, it seemed to be more dangerous than that. Nathan felt the same as her, the intensity of what they had between them already after only a couple of days was difficult to confront and risky.

Kim wanted to believe him, she wanted his intentions to be good but she was too afraid. Nathan understood her apprehension. She was a girl who was scarred, but Kim would never admit that. He too got into bed and turned to face her back. He knew she wasn't asleep, but also was aware of the fact that Kim needed some space. There was nothing else he could do right then to make her trust him and what he was saying.

He just wished the night had gone a completely different way.

Chapter 17

"C'mon Nathan, you knew what I was saying was completely right."

"No it wasn't Stephen. I can't even explain how pissed I am at you right now." Nathan grumbled.

"I just want to make sure your head is in the right place. You've waited so long to get revenge for everything Green has done to you, don't mess this up all because of some girl you've screwed couple of times. Why does it even matter if she took what I said the wrong way? Why should you care?"

"Because..." He hesitated for a moment, not quite sure whether to tell his friend the complete truth or not. "Because she's been hurt too many times before. I don't want to just be another asshole that makes an appearance in her life and screws things up completely for her."

"But your entire mission was to bring her back to D.C to the CIA. If you don't think that's screwing things up for her then I don't know what is-"

"I think- I think I'm having a change of mind." Nathan said hesitantly.

"About what exactly?" Stephen wasn't quite sure what Nathan meant by his words. He was confused and after getting no reply he inquired again. "What are you talking about Nathan?"

"I'm saying that maybe I won't bring her to D.C. Maybe she's better off somewhere else? I'm afraid of what they might do to her. Kim doesn't deserve whatever she has coming for her."

"I thought she was a conniving little rich kid who created software to hack the US Government's computers? That doesn't sound like she is undeserving of what's ahead of her to me."

"It's not like that. Things are a lot different than I had expected. My immediate thoughts about her are completely different to what she is actually like in person. She's different."

What Nathan was saying was the complete truth. Kim had turned out to be an entirely different person to what he had expected at first. He had accepted that now although it was difficult to take in at the beginning. Kim was not the bad person in this situation, she was foolish, but she was not evil. His interpretation had been twisted by his own negativity but he had figured out by then that she was more good than bad.

"I just hope you're making all of the right decisions here Nathan. I know you think I'm a dick for being this way but it's because I'm your friend and it's because I care about you. I don't think you've fully thought all of this through. Planning on running away with a girl you know next to nothing about and putting her before the revenge you've been seeking for twelve years is definitely not the right choice. But it's your own choice and I suppose I have to accept that. It just makes me wonder how special she really is. You have never been so affected by a woman like this before in a long time."

"I'm not exactly putting her before my revenge against Green. We're going to poison him, we're going to kill him and settle the score. I'm just not using Kim as a pawn in my plan. Anyways, I have to go. She's waiting for me back at the hotel." Stephen rolled his eyes in response but said nothing. "I'll see you later tonight for drinks."

"See you later man."

They said their goodbyes and soon enough Nathan was on his way back to the hotel. He went out for lunch with Stephen to talk about Friday night's event. He originally planned for Kim to go along too but she refused to leave their suite. She said she wasn't going somewhere with him to just sit there and be dismissed every time she opened her mouth.

Although Nathan knew it was a bad idea leaving her there, he could not drag her to go with him. But later that day, he had something planned for them that he thought she might enjoy. Since their argument the night before, Kim was deflated and unenthusiastic. She was confused and unsure whether to begin trusting Nathan again, she decided to just snap at him every time he spoke instead.

He knew he messed up, Kim was beginning to open up to him and Stephen's words sent her right back into her shell again. Surprisingly to him, she was lounging on the sofa watching a movie when he got back. Nathan shook off his jacket and then walked into the living room area to see she hadn't even acknowledged his arrival.

"Kim."

"Nathan." She replied curtly, her eyes remaining glued to the screen in front of her.

"We're going out in an hour or two. Go get ready."

"No."

"Kim," he urged and sat down in the armchair closest to her. "Look at me." She rolled her eyes and then turned her gaze to him.

"What?" she asked.

"I know you're still pissed but we're going somewhere special. You're going to love it."

"As much as I love spending time with you?" she replied, rather dryly.

"Even more, if that's possible."

Kim didn't reply to him, only got up off of the couch and went to get ready. She took her time, hoping it would annoy him but he was being more than a little patient with her. Nathan didn't want to fight any more. He wanted her to believe him and also, he wanted to make it up to her. If things went back to the way they were, he would be delighted although he knew that would be difficult to achieve with a girl like Kim. Second chances, if any at all were rare.

Within a couple of minutes in the car, Nathan and Kim were stopping next to a theatre. Kim didn't want to get her hopes up, and so followed Nathan inside without saying a word.

"What are we doing here?" she asked quietly.

"We're going to see Peter Pan, the ballet, dumbass. Didn't you see the sign?" Nathan joked.

The excitement and delight Kim felt in that moment was too much for her to hide any long, the cocktail of both emotions made her forget her worries that emerged from last night's conversation with Stephen. She giggled at him, unable to think of a witty comeback. He enjoyed seeing her smile again, he loved watching the excitement appear on her face and he relished the sound of her laughter because of him.

Kim hadn't seen a ballet in what felt like years by then. Although she was not dancing in this one, she would thoroughly enjoy watching it. Nathan reached out and took her hand before walking to the ticket office. The reception area was full of people who chatted rather loudly all around. She didn't shake out of his grip, remembering how she missed his touch, even a small one like this.

It had been less than twenty-four hours since their argument and she was already missing him, despite his presence all day. She guessed she just wanted things to go back to the way they were, and decide just then that they would, but she wouldn't forget what she heard over dinner last night. Kim would watch out for him, although she didn't want to admit his denial of the accusations she made felt like the complete truth.

They sat and watched the ballet together. Nathan wasn't particularly interested in it but liked watching how she lit up once her eyes looked at the stage. The dancers swirled around and gracefully took over the stage, the joy Kim felt only subsided at the realisation that she may never dance like that on stage again. And so, as they left the theatre to make their way to Nathan's car, he couldn't ignore her frowning face any longer.

The mood seemed to have faltered, even Nathan was fully aware of how disheartened she became. Kim spoke very little on the drive but opened her mouth to talk once she noticed they were not returning home just yet.

"Where are you taking me now?"

"We're meeting Stephen for drinks. We won't be too long Kim."

"Alright." Kim felt deflated and too taken away by her sad thoughts to argue with him.

Once inside the club, they met with Stephen who was sitting at a table waiting for them. Kim barely said two words to either men for a couple of minutes until Nathan volunteered to go and get a round of drinks. She couldn't help but feel uncomfortable alone with Stephen, who was chirpy and polite to her once she arrived, although she did not even spare him a glance and ignored him when he greeted her. She was unable to get his remarks out of her mind.

"Listen, I know you think I'm an asshole right now. You have every reason to think that but you don't understand." Stephen finally spoke. Kim had been looking away but then turned to catch eyes with him, giving him her full attention then.

"I'm not Nathan's play thing." She said in a stone cold voice. "So get that out of your head."

"I know, he's given me enough shit for my poor choice of words already-"

"I don't care what he's done. I'm just telling you myself."

"Please don't be mad at me because of that, I take it back. It's just that- it all seemed a little strange to me."

"What did?" she asked, quite surprised that she was actually having a conversation with him after she promised she would give him as little attention as possible.

"Nathan changing his mind about the entire plan because of you. I don't mean to be rude but you're just a girl and he's been looking for revenge for almost twelve years now."

"I get it, you don't have to remind me." She rolled her eyes at his statement about her. Kim didn't know whether to feel relieved that she would never end up with Nathan or not, she wasn't sure whether she wanted to just be 'a girl' to him or not.

"He's my best friend, he has been since we were young kids. I care about him. So when he shows up to Las Vegas with a change of plan because of a woman, I obviously start to get suspicious. I want this mission to work out for him, after all that's happened to him, he deserves to get Kevin Green back. I was just looking out for him, I don't want him to screw this up because of who he is actually screwing." Stephen's honesty made Kim like him just a little bit more that night. She had gone from disliking him to understanding where he was coming from.

"I'm glad Nathan has a friend like you. He needs someone to look out for him after everything."

"So he's told you- everything?" Kim furrowed her brows at him in confusion. It was then that Stephen realised he said too much.

"He told me about his parents being murdered yes. Is there anything else?" Stephen gulped and tried his very best not to look suspicious.

"No, nothing else." He lied, his words transparent.

"I know you're lying." she narrowed her eyes at him.

"Listen, there's other things in Nathan's past that he obviously doesn't want to share with you. You have to understand and respect his privacy."

Kim had practically poured her heart out to Nathan about everything from her past, except for what happened between Shane and her friends, and so was shocked upon discovering he had left out parts of his.

"So there is something else then?"

"I can't answer that. If he wants you to know, you'll know. Nathan's a very difficult man to talk to about his past. He's broken but he won't ever admit it. Not to me and not to you."

"Please, can't you just tell me a small bit?"

In that moment, Stephen contemplated on whether to tell Kim the awful tragedy that Nathan had to face just a couple of years after both his mother and father were taken away from him. Kim was obviously not just like the rest of the girls Nathan would take an interest in for a little while.

Stephen was not stupid, he knew that their situation was difficult because of how they had met and the mission Nathan had to complete. But for his friend to even consider going against the CIA's instructions for Kim made Stephen more than a little skeptical. Was he allowing someone into his heart again after all of these years? And would it be with a girl who was the most difficult to keep considering the circumstances with the CIA? He wasn't quite sure he knew the answers to those questions yet, but one thing he did know was that Kim must have meant something to Nathan. He cared, and Stephen knew it. So making a decision to tell Kim another part of Nathan's past, a part she might never know unless Stephen told her himself, was difficult.

But Nathan was scarred, and Kim needed to know that in case she was the type of girl who played games.

"Just don't fuck around with him okay? He might seem strong at times but things can still hurt him. He needs to be in control a lot, it makes him feel better because of how little power he had over all the other shit in his life." Kim wasn't quite sure what to say for a moment, she was taken aback. She was about to question him further but he cut across her again.

"Wh-"

"Let's just say Nathan's parents aren't the only ones Kevin Green took away from him."

Before any more words could be exchanged, Nathan had arrived back and was placing their drinks on the table. Kim pushed her and Stephen's conversation to the back of her mind then, but wouldn't forget it. The three got along a lot better after that, all of them interacted with each other. Nathan was surprised by the fact that Stephen and Kim were getting along but said nothing about it, until they were on their way home in the car alone.

"You shouldn't be driving?" Kim said, she was a little drunk from the couple of drinks she had but wasn't completely wasted.

"I was drinking coke Kim, do you really think I'd actually get behind the wheel if I was drunk?"

"Oh." She said quietly. "I didn't know."

"Someone has to look after you if you get too drunk." He chuckled a little. "Hey what were you and Stephen talking about earlier?" Nathan asked her casually.

"He just apologised."

"I guessed so, considering before I left you two you wouldn't even breathe in his direction."

"I can be a stubborn girl sometimes."

"Don't I know." He replied before turning into the parking lot.

It took them very little time to get up to their room. The mood had changed quickly once they were in the privacy of their suite. Kim got into one of Nathan's t-shirts and climbed into bed to find a shirtless Nathan already in there, lying on his side to face her.

She gulped at the sight of him. Although she had seen him like this many times before, she felt shyness creep up on her. Nathan reached out and traced patterns on her arm while she watched him carefully.

"Did you enjoy tonight?"

"It would have been better if-"

"If what?"

"If you weren't there." She giggled once she saw him roll his eyes.

"I think I should start taking your insults as compliments at this stage Kim."

"Maybe you should yes." There was a short silence before she spoke again, this time her voice was quiet and gentle. She looked him in the eye, "Thanks for today Nathan, the ballet was amazing."

"Not as amazing as me surely?"

Kim laughed again, but could say no more because soon enough Nathan's lips were tormenting hers, soft and gentle, slow and sultry. It seemed so sudden yet what she was craving all night. She pulled away for a moment to look at him; his gaze was intense and almost questioning. She knew why, she knew he was looking for her to say yes to him again, she knew he was looking for her forgiveness.

And for a moment, Kim was unsure as to whether kissing him back was the right thing to do or not, but then she decided she couldn't hold against him for long. Kim believed Nathan when he told her he wasn't using sex as a way to trick her into being a part of his plan.

When she kissed him back, she just hoped it was the right decision.

Chapter 18

Kim couldn't sleep at all that night. She managed to shake out of Nathan's arms and put some clothes on before making her way quietly out to the balcony. It was five in the morning but Las Vegas was still truly awake. She looked out at the beautiful view of bright lights before her while Stephen's words continued to invade her thoughts: Nathan's parents aren't the only ones Kevin Green took away from him.

The realisation that there was more misfortune to Nathan's already tragic story made Kim's chest ache. She felt more sympathy for him than anyone she had ever met before. It crushed her to wonder what else may have happened to him, and how much more he had to deal with in his past. All of this made her realise that she truly did care about Nathan, as much as she didn't want to believe that, it was the truth.

She had been up all night worrying about him and trying to figure out how much more there was to his story. Her head hurt, her eyes itched with hunger for sleep and her heart felt heavy in her chest. She brought her knees to her chest and rested her chin on them before letting out a deep breath.

All of a sudden, Kim felt another weight on her chest. She remembered Stephen's warning about not hurting him and couldn't overlook it. Maybe she didn't mean enough to Nathan to be able to hurt him, but she knew for sure what they had between them certainly would. The realisation came after she thought about all of this running around and jumping into bed with one another they would soon enough end up in D.C and never speak again. Maybe their relationship that wasn't really a relationship needed to be nipped in the bud before any feelings grew stronger.

"Hey." Kim almost jumped at the sound of Nathan's voice, barely above a whisper. He too had thrown some clothes on and was standing at the door of the balcony observing at her.

"Hey." She smiled at him, although she really didn't feel like smiling. Nathan sensed her sorrow and took a seat across from her, wondering what was wrong. "I'm sorry, did I wake you? You should probably go back to bed."

"No it's fine really. I woke up and noticed you were gone."

"It's beautiful isn't it?" Kim eyed the view ahead of her again for a moment before looking back at him.

"It sure is." It took him a minute or two to turn his head to face her again and once his eyes connected with hers, he spoke. "Is something wrong?" He seemed concerned, she hesitated then.

"I don't think we should do this anymore." Kim eventually spit out what was on her mind and instantly noticed the expression of hurt creep up on his features. He was confused.

"What? Why?" he remained calm but couldn't quite understand why she was saying the things she was saying.

"Nathan, you know there are a million things wrong with what we're both doing. It's not that I don't want to I, I just don't think it's the best idea-"

"But it's just sex, remember?" he recalled the same words she had used in the beginning of all of this.

"I know I just- I don't want either of us to get hurt."

"We won't." he looked her dead in the eye then, both still remaining relaxed.

"I just keep thinking that after all of this, we're going to have to go to D.C and then that will be it. And I don't know about you, but that makes me feel... different than I expected."

"Well what if we didn't go to D.C?" his words made her hold her breath and inspect him with her eyes for signs that this was a joke.

"You wouldn't do that."

"How do you know?"

"Because that's ridiculous. As much as I don't want to face whatever it is I'm going to face when I get there, you'd never agree to just run away with me- again."

"I'm not so sure anymore Kim. I think that maybe we shouldn't go to D.C, just until I figure out a plan."

"A plan?" she asked, confused.

"A plan to prove you're innocent. To prove that you're father tricked you into making the software."

"You would do that for me?"

"Yes." Nathan's tone told her that there wasn't any other answer. It all felt a bit strange.

"I can't just keep running away."

"Sometimes running away is the best way to deal with your problems." His words were deep with meaning; it felt as though he was talking from previous experience along with her situation.

"I- I don't know what to say." She really was lost for words.

"Then don't say anything at all." His voice was gentle and for once, Kim listened to him.

Next of all, Nathan stood up and sat beside her on the outdoor love seat. He tugged her close to his chest and wrapped his arms around her, the familiar sweet smell and feeling of her presence was comforting for him and his thoughts.

This couldn't be the best option, but then again, going straight to D.C didn't feel like a particularly amazing plan either. Maybe she was prolonging her time with him instead of facing what needed to be faced with the CIA but she didn't care right then, just snuggled closer to Nathan. He nuzzled her neck and took in her scent. There was a comfortable silence between the pair for a little while until Kim spoke, wanting to change the topic of conversation to something lighter.

"Want to play twenty questions?" she turned her head slightly to look up at him and saw him chuckle, feeling his chest vibrate on her back.

"Alright then."

"If you could be anything at all, other than a CIA agent, what would you be?" she asked, curiosity taking over.

"That's easy." He said shortly after she finished her question. "I'd work at McDonald's." Nathan deadpanned, followed by Kim erupting into blissful laughter. It was like music to his ears then, he savoured it completely.

"You know, I could see you working there actually. The uniform would look great on you."

"Kim anything could look great on me. You could put me in a bin liner and I'd still be fuckable."

"God, you're insane." She rolled her eyes before grinning like an idiot. "Although there's nothing at all wrong with working in McDonald's, I doubt you're being serious so I need an actual answer since I'm wasting my question on it."

"I'm not sure. I always wanted to do this. I mean, when I was younger I was very good at football but not good enough to go anywhere with it."

"Was it not difficult when you were younger and your parents were working? I'm sure their missions would probably be very long."

"They began working normal hours with more office type work after they had me. They decided it was the best thing to do."

"Oh, I see."

"Right, my turn. Since you asked two in a row, I get to do the same."

"If you could have a super power, what would it be?"

"I think I'd like to be able to fly. Or no, maybe it would be good to read people's minds. Or-"

"You have to pick one." He chuckled.

"No, I'll just stick with flying."

"Okay, question ten... What's your favourite colour?" Kim paused the very moment his words filled her ears. He did seem genuinely interested, it made her feel happy but she knew it really shouldn't.

"Purple. What's yours?"

"Red."

"Your turn again."

"If you could go anywhere in the world, where would be it?"

"Hmm... that's a difficult one."

"Take your time."

"Hawaii." Nathan scoffed after she answered his question.

"Really?"

"Well who wouldn't want to be in Hawaii right now, I mean c'mon? I know it sounds cliché Nathan but it's my first choice. I've never been."

"Me either." His voice trailed off.

"That's where I'm going to go when all of this shit is over. I'm going to run away to Hawaii." She snuggled closer to him and yawned after she spoke.

Of course, Nathan chuckled at her words. She wasn't being serious, he could tell by her tone. But there was sorrow when she spoke, and that was something that both confused and saddened Nathan at the same time.

"Nathan?" Kim's voice was shaky, it made Nathan snap out of any daze that he was beginning to fall into.

"Yeah?"

"Should I be nervous about tomorrow?"

"No, of course not." His arms tightened around her then involuntarily. Nathan felt a sudden need to protect her.

"Okay."

"Kim?" Nathan said gently as he played with her hair. There were still a couple of unanswered questions eating away at him. He was nosey and too curios for his own good about her.

"Hmm." She mumbled. He could tell then that she was getting tired.

"Do you miss anyone?" Nathan wasn't exactly asking about Chicago, the question was about Portland too.

"I'm not sure." Kim said after a long pause.

"What do you mean?"

"Well, I don't know whether there is a point in missing people that are out of my reach. I don't know how my life is going to go from here, but I certainly don't think it's going to go back to normal again. My friends in Portland were great, but I haven't really been thinking about them. My friendship with them was different to the ones I had when I lived back in Chicago."

"In what way?"

"In lots of ways. The friends I had back in Chicago were completely different to the ones I made in Portland. I knew all of them my whole life -well I thought I knew them."

"What's that supposed to mean?"

"They left me really disappointed."

"Because they wouldn't move away with you?"

"Can we talk about something else now?" Kim failed miserably at changing the subject in a subtle way but hoped he wouldn't keep urging her to explain her reasons for hating her old friends.

Although Nathan knew there was something particularly fishy about the entire thing, he did as she asked and stayed quiet. The fact that whenever Kim's friends were mentioned, she was always holding back, and keeping this big secret from him about them made him even more interested despite knowing he probably would never get the information out of her.

Nathan thought that whatever it was her friends had done, it was something unforgiveable and difficult to talk about. But what Nathan didn't know was that unforgiveable thing also had something to do with Shane. Kim almost cringed at the thought of explaining to Nathan the story of how she lost her best friends and her boyfriend at the same time. She didn't forgive or forget, and that was understandable considering the circumstances.

"Maybe we should go to bed." Nathan finally spoke. He could hear her breaths begin to get heavier by the minute and knew she was probably falling back to sleep.

"Hmm." She answered again in that same sleep tone like before.

"C'mon. Kim." He whispered in her ear and shook her a little but she didn't budge.

It took him some time to get up off of the love seat since she had been lying on him. Once he did so, he picked her up gently and began to carry her.

"Nathan." She groaned.

"Shut up Kim, you're lucky I didn't make you walk to bed."

"You shut up." Kim's voice was soft and relaxed, her words made him laugh a little.

"We have a busy day ahead of us tomorrow, so we need to sleep in an actual bed and not on the balcony of our hotel room."

Nathan put her down in bed and got in beside her. Kim felt his weight on the bed and moved closer to him under the covers.

"Night Nathan." She whispered before falling back to sleep again, this time her mind a little more at ease from the conversation with Nathan. Although her mind still wandered into all of the endless possibilities of what Stephen's words could have meant earlier, Nathan's arms were comforting enough to make her forget for a little while.

In the short couple of minutes Kim had before she fell asleep, she realised she was not the only one of the pair that had been hurt badly. She decided it was time to treat Nathan a little nicer than before, he too had been through a lot and still was trying to make her feel better. Bringing her to the ballet had been a perfect example. Kim needed to give him a break, and she promised to do so tomorrow.

Meanwhile Nathan was almost panicking about his feelings towards Kim. As he held her close, his arms wrapped tightly around her, he felt at ease, he felt relaxed and context. But most of all he felt terrified because Kim was dangerous for his heart, and she didn't even know it yet.

Chapter 19

"**I**f your favourite colour is red, why couldn't I wear it tonight?" Kim called from inside the bathroom.

Nathan was straightening his tie in the mirror beside their bed when he heard her and rolled his eyes immediately.

"Are you still going on about that dress from a couple days ago?" There was humour in his tone, he found it funny but nerves were beginning to kick in for him and what he had planned for that night. He wondered what Kim would think, but tried his very best to put her to the back of his mind for the time being. But forgetting about her for a night was proving to be extremely difficult, especially after she came out of the bathroom, ready to go.

She looked breathtakingly beautiful. Of course, that was an opinion Nathan would keep to himself. But he could not hide his reaction when catching the first sight of her, all set for the night ahead of them.

Kim's hair was up, her recently purchased make up was flawless and her dress clung to her skin in a way that made her even more irresistible to Nathan. It wasn't just her looks, it was everything about her that made her truly captivating to him- it was something he could not embrace. Nathan found it quite scary actually, how he felt around her.

"I don't like this one." She frowned a little, at first she was looking at him but as soon as the words escaped her mouth, she diverted her gaze to the ground.

"What? Why not?" Nathan quickly walked towards her in order to stand next to her.

"Nothing, never mind. I'm just nervous. Forget I said anything." Kim insisted before walking briskly to the other side of the room to grab her purse.

Nathan followed her and put his hands around her waist in order to keep her near. He kissed her on the lips tenderly and once they broke away, he rested his forehead on hers for a moment.

"Don't be nervous. We're just going to this event, I'm going to handle Green and then we're going to go somewhere else for the night. You have nothing to be worried about, okay?" he reassured her, looking into her eyes. Kim only gave him a nod in response but smiled then once she caught sight of his reassuring smile.

"Let's go." He took her hand and the two left together.

The resort where the function was being held was massive. The casino's bright flashing lights and the huge amount of people that turned up were the perfect distraction that night for Nathan's plan.

The pair arrived in the lobby of the resort and looked around for a couple of minutes to find Stephen. Once the three said their hellos, they went in to the event taking place. The casino in the hotel was buzzing with excitement and eagerness although it didn't appeal to Kim in the slightest. She sipped on her drink and watched as both Stephen and Nathan played a couple games of blackjack. Kim noticed Nathan was being a little off with her, but decided if there was a problem, she would wait to address it the next morning. She didn't want to be the reason any of Nathan's revenge plans were messed up so stayed quiet about it.

It wasn't until the two men spotted Kevin Green on the other side of the huge casino, that things took their turn for the worst in Kim's eyes regarding Nathan's behaviour. Stephen nudged his friend and spoke in a hushed tone to him, but Kim could still just about make out what was being said.

"So you still haven't told me how you're going to pull this off. What are we going to do now?" he asked. The three of them had sat down and were enjoying their drinks when Nathan decided to tell Kim and Stephen of his new plan, but it seemed to turn up right before their eyes, he was unable to get the words out first.

"Hello Nathan." Kim's eyes diverted to a young woman standing in front of their table. She watched like a hawk as Nathan immediately got up from his seat to greet her. His hands went around her waist as he brought her towards him for a hug before she kissed his cheek and smiled flirtatiously at him.

Kim couldn't help but glower in silence at the stranger who seemed to be very fond of Nathan. Stephen noticed her sudden change in mood and watched carefully.

"This is Felicity. Felicity, these are my two friends Stephen and Kim." Kim's head snapped towards Nathan's direction at the word friend. She couldn't help the burning jealousy she was feeling right then although she knew she was being completely ridiculous. "You look beautiful tonight." Nathan said close to Felicity's ear while Kim pretended she hadn't heard.

"Hello." Felicity smiled at the two who were sitting down. Kim gave her a nod and took another sip of her drink while she took in Felicity's appearance.

She was wearing a red dress that accentuated her curves in the right way. Nathan was right, Kim thought deciding to be brutally honest with herself, this other woman did look amazing. More amazing than Kim would ever look.

"This is my new plan. Felicity is going to do the job for me." Nathan finally announced once all four were sitting down again.

"Oh really?" Stephen quirked an eyebrow at his friend.

"Yes and as soon as it's done, she'll give us a signal. We'll slip out calmly without drawing too much attention and then we can go somewhere else." He spoke with finality and control.

Nathan noticed how quiet Kim had gotten, his eyes caught onto hers for a moment but she only nodded in response, appearing to be in her own world at that moment in time. He knew he was testing her patience that night, but he wanted to see how far he could go before she said anything about it. He found the brooding Kim quite funny to take in and continued on with his act.

Soon enough, Felicity was leaving their table and blending in amongst the crowds of people. Nathan's eyes followed her intently as she swanned around the room with elegance, finally reaching Kevin Green who was sitting at the bar.

"Is this going to take long?" Kim asked, hoping her true emotions wouldn't be evident in her voice.

"Let's hope not. She seems to be doing a good job at luring him in anyways." Stephen was the one to give her a reply.

"I need another drink." She said before getting up and going to a bar nearest their table.

"So Felicity huh?" Stephen eyed Nathan with curiosity before continuing. "I didn't know you two still talked."

"We bump into each other now and then." Nathan's poker face was on.

"And what made you decide to bring her in on this?"

"She's an agent too; she deals with this kind of stuff all the time. I didn't want Kim involved in any of this, for her own good. I need to make sure she's okay."

"You don't seem to be acting that way tonight?" Stephen shot back, rather daringly. It made Nathan stop looking across the room and turn to his friend then.

"Don't start Stephen."

"What? I'm being honest. Sure, you needed Felicity to be a part of this but the way you're behaving with her is a whole different story."

"It's my own business, not yours."

"I'm just saying. I don't think you should be playing any games with Kim, which is exactly what you're planning on doing. If you want to make sure she's okay then why be like this in front of her?"

"Since when do you care about what's between me and Kim?"

"I don't I'm just saying-"

"Well don't." Nathan narrowed his eyes at the other man. Kim returned to their table, meaning the conversation immediately turned to something else.

It didn't take much time before Felicity gave Nathan the signal and all of them were heading back to Kim and Nathan's hotel. The casino was huge there too, and also as crowded as the other one. They played a couple games, and placed some bets to pass the night away. Throughout that time, Kim felt as though she couldn't take it anymore. Nathan seemed to be with Felicity all night. He didn't even spare Kim a second glance. Because of this, she stuck with Stephen for the night.

"Nathan." Kim called him, tugging at his sleeve to get his attention. He was clearly annoyed at being torn away from his conversation with Felicity.

"What?" he asked, his voice harsh and stern.

"Can I talk to you for a minute?" she remained her usual self, she wouldn't let it show how upset she was becoming and that was the reason Nathan was taking this so far. He wanted a reaction and was yet to receive one.

Kim wanted to go to bed. She was exhausted and wounded; all she wanted was her extremely comfortable bed upstairs in their extravagant suite.

"Can't it wait 'til tomorrow?" he came across as bored and uninterested. Kim didn't know what to do, but definitely wasn't going to fall at his feet because he was showing interest in another woman. She would make him come crawling back soon enough.

Instead of crying about his harshness, she scowled at him before rolling her eyes.

"Sure." She said through gritted teeth before walking away from the pair.

"Where are you going?" Stephen, who was clearly uncomfortable about the whole thing asked as she walked away.

"I need the bathroom." Kim called over her shoulder.

Once inside, she took a minute to breathe and reflect on what had happened so far that night. Kim was smart enough to realise Nathan was playing a big game with her. She would be the bigger person here and not play into it like he would surely expect her to. He hadn't done anything that was wrong, but the sight of seeing him so close to another woman made her shockingly jealous. She didn't want to be that girl, and so calmed herself down.

Kim needed to keep her composure for the rest of the night. If she reacted at all to Nathan, she knew that would mean he had won and Kim was not a loser. After spending a good five minutes in the bathroom preparing herself for however long she would have to deal with Nathan and Felicity, Kim finally left the toilets and headed back to where she had left everyone else moments ago.

She was surprised to find a lost looking Stephen, sitting awkwardly by himself sipping on a fresh drink. Kim frowned at the sight of him alone and did not sit down.

"Where's Nathan gone?" she asked, a question Stephen had been expecting to be her first.

"They went to get some air." His words were stiff and his tone showed he was clearly fed up.

"I'll be right back-"

"Kim don't bother. Nathan's not being serious about all of this, don't worry about it." Stephen butt in, making her stand in her spot contemplating what her next actions would in fact be. He sighed and looked at her again, waiting for her to say something but instead she turned around and briskly walked away from him.

Kim made her way through all the people in the busy casino and out to the lobby of the hotel. She spotted Nathan straight away, and Felicity of course, in her red dress. But neither had seen her yet. Kim stood in her spot as she looked on with apprehension.

Both were standing outside but could be seen clearly because of the huge floor to ceiling glass windows. Felicity was closer to Nathan than she had been all night but Kim was too far away to spot his uncomfortableness from it. He knew he was tiptoeing on dangerous ground. There was a line that he was choosing not to cross, but it seemed to become a difficult thing to do right then.

Kim watched with complete disappointment as the other woman place soft kisses around Nathan's jaw, each time getting closer and closer to his mouth. He held her but was not pulling her closer nor was he pushing her away.

"Felicity..." he warned, but Kim could obviously not hear.

"Shh." She whispered before hungrily putting her lips on his.

Chapter 20

Kim did not stick around long enough in the lobby to see Nathan pushing Felicity away quickly. She had already turned on her heels and immediately walked back into where Stephen was sitting. He noticed how she seemed to be in a daze and watched her carefully once she sat down.

"Something wrong?"

"Nothing." Within a minute, all of Kim's pep talk she gave to herself was completely forgotten. She moved closer to Stephen. He gulped from the close proximity and also when she placed her hand on his face.

"Kim..."

"Mhm?" her voice was sultry and flirtatious.

"What are you doing?" Stephen didn't know what to do.

"I'm just admiring the view."

"Well why don't you admire it from somewhere else besides my lap?"

"You're so funny Stephen." Kim giggled.

"Cut the bullshit Kim, you know Nathan would cut my dick off if I even showed the slightest interest in you. Don't play into his childish games and get off of me." Kim, who was then draped on his lap in an affectionate display for everyone to see, ignored his stern words.

"Just give me two minutes okay? I want to make him feel the way I've been feeling all god damn night." She began talking normally then, not flirting in any shape or form. She was desperate to get her own back on Nathan.

"You two are crazy and you're making me feel so uncomfortable right now."

Kim frowned to herself. She was glad Nathan had a good friend like Stephen. He clearly had morals and knew when to not cross the line. He would never try to get involved with Kim although what both Nathan and Kim had between them was nothing but sex. Kim just wished she had friends like him when she was back in Chicago. A sadness washed over her as more memories came flooding back. She wasn't good enough for Shane and she certainly wasn't good enough for Nathan either, going by his actions just moments ago.

"Kim? What the hell Kim?" Nathan's angry tone snapped her out of her thoughts. "Stephen get her off of you right now."

Kim didn't move from her spot, only grinned at Nathan in response. Her arm was draped around Stephen's neck and Nathan paid close attention to the contact but noticed how awkward his friend looked.

"Kim." His voice was dark and his eyes burned with fury, leaving a scorching trail wherever they landed. "We're going upstairs." His body was tense and his fists were clenched, his eyes never left hers.

"Fine then." Kim got up off of Stephen to say her goodbyes.

"We'll see you tomorrow." He glared at Stephen then, who held his hands up in surrender.

Nathan took Kim by the wrist and led her out into the lobby. They went straight into an empty elevator. Kim tried to shrug out of his grip he had on her, letting him know she too was angry, but Nathan did not budge. It was only when she glowered at him and spoke, that he let her go.

"Get your fucking dirty hands off of me."

"You weren't saying that last night when they were all over you." He retorted before releasing her wrist.

"Where's Felicity?" she sneered at him, ignoring his previous words because it was only then Kim had realised that Nathan returned to the casino alone.

"She had to go back to her hotel."

"Oh really? I'm surprised you didn't bring her up to our room and fuck her right in front of me. Maybe you'd get a kick out of that too?"

"Shut up." Nathan brushed her off before the elevator doors pinged open and they began walking down the hotel corridor to their suite.

"Don't tell me to shut up." Kim followed behind him, trying to keep up in her heels. "You were practically doing it outside the hotel just a couple minutes ago." She knew she was exaggerating, but she wanted him to know she saw the two of them together. Kim felt it may justify her actions a little bit more.

Nathan stopped putting the key card in the door when the words escaped her mouth. He knew then she had seen Felicity going in for a kiss with him, but what she didn't see was how he then pushed her away. He was not going to explain himself to her; they were nothing to each other so it was not worth his time. Nathan only sighed and opened the door to their room.

The sound of the door slamming shut behind him made his tense body flinch.

"You're over reacting." He stated, turning then to look at Kim who was standing a few steps away from him. He wasn't the only one furious in this argument and he knew she would not let things slip so easily. An argument with Kim was going to be brutal if she was in this mood.

"And you can't say much. You practically dragged me back up here because I was talking to Stephen."

"I wouldn't call it talking Kim. You were sitting on his lap."

"God you're such a hypocrite. At least I wasn't having a make out session with him. And even if I was, that would be none of your business."

"Yes it would. As long as we're together this way, I don't want another man touching you like that. Until we end this, you're mine and mine only." His words sparked a rage within Kim that she could not describe. Indescribable feelings were always the most deadly.

"Let's get this straight Nathan," she neared him, complete indignation filling her. "I'm not yours. I don't belong to any-one but myself so cut the fucking crap. Don't insult me like that again. I'm not an object people can just take possession of whenever they feel like it. And Stephen wasn't touching me in any way-"

"Are you defending him now?" his eyes narrowed, his voice raised a little higher.

"I can't believe you Nathan." Kim raised her voice then too in order to match his. "You're so god damn jealous when nothing happened. You could clearly see Stephen was un-comfortable. How do you think I feel watching you kiss some girl right in front of me? You're such a fucking hypocrite." She said again.

"Nothing happened with Felicity."

"I saw with my own two eyes-"

"We didn't kiss Kim, I pulled away okay?"

"Bullshit." She stated. "I know an unfaithful man when I see one, no wonder you've never had a relationship that lasted very long." Her words wounded him, because she did not know the whole story, on the other hand- it seemed like the penny had dropped for him regarding her past with Shane. And he was not going to let it slide without making a sly remark just like she had.

"Oh don't tell me Shane cheated on you too." Nathan let out a bitter laugh but it was forced. He looked into her eyes then and saw she was just about to break. "You know I wouldn't blame him Kim."

His words dug into her like a knife, she couldn't think of anything else to say yet. He had come at her with a low blow and instead of surrendering; Kim was searching her mind for another insult to attack him with.

She walked over to one of the huge windows in their room and ignored him for a moment. Kim opened the window wide and took in the fresh air. But her attempt at calming herself down wasn't quite working. Nathan was soon close by again.

"Who was it Kim?" His lips grazed her ear and made her involuntarily shiver. "Was it someone you knew?" his voice was callous and cruel. He had hit the last nail in the coffin but Kim had yet to back down. She wanted to cry, she wanted to break down in tears because she was hurt, by Nathan and by Shane all those years ago. Kim wasn't as strong as she made herself out to be, and his words had pushed her past breaking point. "Or maybe it was a complete stranger... Which would make you feel better?" his hands moved to her shoulders, his whispering voice seemed to echo in her mind.

"Go away." She shrugged him off. She didn't want to look at him; she didn't want to say another word. He had won the battle and her pride had been wounded. But instead of backing down, Nathan continued on.

"You became too attached to Shane that you still can't let him go. Now you've become too attached to what we have together but I'm the one in control here Kim." She remembered Stephen's words about Nathan's want for control and decided to stick in a sly dig, although it would be nowhere near as hurtful as the words that were spoken previously that night.

Kim turned around and sniggered at him.

"You blew up tonight because I was sitting on your friend's lap, your friend that you knew would never try anything with me and that you knew was obviously uncomfortable by my advances on him. While I had every right to be angry because you kissed some girl that definitely didn't look like she was uncomfortable from the close contact. I think you're the one who's become too attached Nathan." Her words woke him up a little but he didn't know how to respond. "And I also think if anyone is in control here, it's me."

The realisation had sunk in with him the second the words escaped her lips. He looked her dead in the eye, and within a short moment, Kim knew she had pushed him too far. Anger washed over every feature on his face. He charged at her and grabbed her tightly before leaning her out of the open window.

Kim screamed at first, the shock not being able to subside. She struggled under his grip he had on her. She was terrified of what he might do next. Nathan's eyes burned with anger and he did not speak for a moment.

"I'm the only one in control Kim." He spoke through gritted teeth. "Now say it, say it!"

"Nathan! Stop. Please Nathan-"

"Fucking say it Kim." As he stood there, Nathan had a sudden realisation that he did care about Kim. Although discovering this in the twisted circumstances, he knew that there was no way he could let her go. He knew that whether she said what he wanted her to say or not, she was going to be safe.

"You're the one in control!" She finally spit out the words that Nathan thought would sound gratifying but instead, they made his chest constrict. Kim almost felt disappointed in herself for giving in, but the look in his eyes made her think he would let her plummet to her death out of the window if she had've waited a minute longer. He quickly allowed her to stand up again but her legs couldn't hold her up.

Kim sunk to the ground, terrible tears pricking her eyes. Her expression showed shock and disbelief, she could not process fully what just happened. The two looked at each other with incredulity, neither saying a single word yet. At first Kim was angry, but then, she decided she was more disappointed than she was furious.

"You've gotten your reaction you've been waiting for all night." Kim was calmer than calm. Her features and voice seemed to be lacking any emotion. It scared Nathan to see her like that. The instant regret had kicked in within himself, he wished he had stayed calmer and not done such a foolish thing to try and prove himself. If anything, it had proved he did in fact care about Kim, a lot more than he expected at first.

The thought of letting her go a moment ago crushed him into what felt like a million pieces. If she had fallen out of the window, he knew he would jump right out after her. The frightening realisation of this made him want to take it all back, everything he had done the entire night. But Kim was not one to take apologies so easily. Her forgiveness was something he wished was within his reach but he knew better by then.

"Kim-"

"Don't say anything else. I don't want to speak to you right now. This playful back and forth we've been having has gone too far. I'm done, I'm over it." She said before standing up and walking away, Nathan hot on her tail.

Kim made her way to the bedroom and slammed the door right in his face. Nathan decided the best option may be to sleep on one of the couches that night. But once he had tried to get comfortable, he felt restless. His thoughts were tormenting him but he could not help it.

He really liked Kim. He loved her sassiness and how she didn't care sometimes. He liked it when she was stroppy and bossy and how unapologetic she was about everything and anything at all. It seemed strange, to like parts of someone's personality that were supposed to be disliked, but he could not change it and if he could, he would not choose to do so.

Nathan was fucked up, he was twisted and foolish. He liked Kim but was treating her as if she was his worst enemy.

It took him a long time to fall asleep that night, the same could be said for Kim too.

Chapter 21

Kim woke up to the sound of someone moving around the bedroom. Her eyes, full of sleep cracked open to find Nathan placing a huge tray on the bed beside her with food on it. Kim rolled over onto her back and sat up a little in bed.

"I ordered room service for you." Nathan's voice was sweeter than she had ever heard before.

The guilt had really consumed him entirely last night. He was up until the early hours of the morning, analysing everything that happened the night before. He felt a terrible cocktail of shame and guilt because of everything he did but didn't know how he was going to make it up to Kim.

By then, Nathan had fully established the fact that he cared a great deal for Kim. If he didn't, his mind would not have gone into over drive trying to think of how many ways he could show her he was sorry. There could be no denying that although their relationship was physical, Nathan felt more than simple attraction for her. He was not afraid to admit that to himself anymore, but was extremely concerned by the fact that he probably messed up everything for good.

If the argument last night hadn't have escalated, the two would feel somewhat even and it would be easier to move on from that. But it wasn't. Nathan had threatened her life, he had done this in an attempt to deny what he was truly feeling. His plan only had the opposite effect, by showing him he liked Kim, a lot more than he let on. Although he knew he could never let her fall to her death out of the window he hung her out of, Kim did not know that and certainly would not believe him if he told her otherwise.

"I'm not hungry." She lied. Her voice was gruff but her facial expression was no different than the one she supported last night. It lacked much emotion and scared him.

"I made sure your eggs were scrambled, I know how much you liked them the last time we ordered breakfast."

"I don't care. I don't want it." Kim replied straight away, her words made his chest hurt.

Nathan sighed and sat down on the edge of the bed beside her. She silently refused to look directly at him.

"Please Kim."

"You think one fucking breakfast is going to make me feel better?" She knew he was not urging her to eat the breakfast he brought her, but was asking for forgiveness.

"No, this is just the start of everything. I'm going to make it up to you I-"

"Make it up to me? I already told you Nathan, I'm the most unforgiving person you'll ever meet. You get one chance, if you mess up that's it." He remembered that conversation very clearly. "Why would you want to make it up to me anyway?" she scoffed. Nathan hesitated for a moment before speaking.

"Because I care about you." He admitted although he knew he was setting himself up for rejection. Kim was a closed book, she would probably never let him in again.

"Is openly flirting all night and kissing another woman always your way of showing how much you care about someone? Because if it is, I think you may be doing the wrong thing."

"You were openly flirting with Stephen too."

"But I'm not the one who's admitting they care." She had a valid point. There was a silence in the room for a minute or two until Nathan spoke again.

"And I didn't kiss her. She tried to kiss me but I pulled away. It's not my fault that she-"

"Nathan, don't put the blame on Felicity. Even if I believed all that 'I didn't kiss her, she kissed me' shit, you gave her every sign to make her believe you were going to kiss her back by your actions all night. You were setting yourself up for disaster if you didn't want her to make advances on you." Nathan couldn't understand why he was not blowing up right then in a rage. She was winning this discussion and he hated it- but everything she was saying was completely correct. "And I don't care about that anymore. If you cared about me, you wouldn't have dangled me out of a twenty story building until I told you how in control you were. That's fucked up."

"I'm a fucked up person."

"I'm a fucked up person too. That doesn't give you any validation."

"Kim you're being ridiculous." He said in exasperation.

"I'm not ridiculous, I'm just not delusional." She said before getting up out of bed. "What you did was wrong, quit while you're ahead." Kim called over her shoulder before entering the bathroom.

"Get ready, we're going to meet Stephen-"

"I'm not going anywhere with you until we're on the road back to D.C." she said from the other side of the door. It was obvious Kim would rather face whatever was coming her way if she went to D.C than run away for a little while with Nathan then.

Nathan let out a sigh, she had left him mulling over their conversation in the bedroom alone.

"Listen, before you say a word- I didn't try anything with Kim okay? I wouldn't do that. So if you want to-"

"Stephen shut up for a second, there's much more serious things at hand here..." Nathan's voice was thick with annoyance and frustration.

"What's wrong?" The other man asked, showing some concern for his friend.

"Kim."

"What about Kim?"

"I messed up last night. She's never going to forgive me, what the hell am I going to do?"

"Why are you so surprised? You could clearly see you were pissing her off all night?"

"No..." Nathan took a breath before he looked up at Stephen and began to speak. "I done something else too." He stated.

It took him a couple of minutes to explain everything from the night before to Stephen. He told him about Felicity and how she had tried to kiss him. Stephen had rolled his eyes at the mention of her name and explained to Nathan how bad that may have looked from Kim's perspective.

Nathan went on to inform Stephen about the whole window incident and how he was up all night thinking of ways to make it up to Kim.

"I guess you're screwed man. That's just fucked up." Stephen said.

"Thanks for the help."

"Hey," he held his hands up in a surrender gesture, "I'm just being honest. There's nothing you can do about it."

"But there has to be." There was a short silence for a moment or two while Stephen sat, analysing everything his friend had told him.

"Why did you do it Nathan?"

"I'm not quite sure." He hesitated.

"There has to be some reason. You don't just threaten someone's life for no reason at all."

"I guess anger took over me. I would never have actually gone through with it, I just wanted to scare her because I just- I just got so angry. I was shouting and so was she, we both said stupid things to hurt each other. But I guess she pushed me too far. She didn't understand, I know she didn't and in that moment, I didn't care. It was like a low blow that she never even knew existed. I guess that's my fault for not telling her."

"What did she say to you?" he needed to know, but wondered why he should even ask. It took only a small number of things to throw Nathan over the edge completely.

"Just some things..."

"Nathan." Stephen sighed loudly before looking at the visible pain displayed on Nathan's face. "Was it about Madison?" he tried his very best to ease gently into the topic, although that seemed impossible to do at the best of times.

"I said a lot of stupid shit to her, about her boyfriend and stuff. She told me it didn't surprise her that I could never keep a relationship for that long, that kind of got the ball rolling yes. She said she was in control, and I knew she was right. I knew there was nothing I could do about it right then either, because I feel like it's happening again- just like with Madison- and once I don't have control bad things happen."

"Nathan you have to stop blaming yourself, you can't carry around all this shit with you for the rest of your life."

"Madison was the love of my life Stephen." Nathan said with frustration. "I know you can't seem to understand because you haven't met yours yet but I have. And she's not right here now because of me." He buried his face in his hands for a moment.

"You've gotten your own back on Kevin Green now, I know it isn't the same-"

"I wish revenge felt better than this but it doesn't. Kevin Green ordered my parents to be murdered and then four years later, the love of my life. Sure, I killed him but it doesn't bring anyone back, it just opens the wounds again. The only reason Madison is dead is because I couldn't stay in control, I let her take charge because I loved her with all my heart. I should have let her go, I should have pushed her away so that I never fell for her but I didn't. And I can never forgive myself for that. Maybe it's better that Kim doesn't forgive me, maybe then she won't ever get hurt by whoever else is around the corner waiting to make my life a living hell."

"Nathan-"

"No, it doesn't matter. I don't want to talk about Madison, I don't want to talk about any of this anymore can we change the topic please."

"Why don't you just explain to Kim?"

"Because I can't. You know how hard it is for me to talk about it with even the people closest to me. I can't tell her. Not right now anyway."

"So you do plan on telling her some time?" there was a long silence while Nathan thought about his options.

"I'm not sure okay? Now can we talk about something else."

The conversation changed to something entirely different like Nathan had hoped. They sat together for another while before Nathan decided it would be best to go back to his hotel to check on Kim. He was surprised to find her sitting out on the balcony, looking at the beautiful view they had seen just a night or two ago together.

Kim had a lot of time to think while Nathan was out and had come up with a plan she found best to use when he returned home. She thought a lot about what her next move would be, she just knew she couldn't stay here with him- whether she was putting herself in danger or not. Kim realised she cared a lot about Nathan despite everything that had happened, despite knowing there were so many reasons she shouldn't. And when he threatened her life, in order to make himself feel more in control, it had made Kim feel more than she had ever expected.

She wanted him to care about her too, although the thought was ridiculous. Kim was no fool. Nathan's words could not erase his actions and an apology would not be accepted on her behalf. She needed to get out of there, she needed to go before she was hurt any more. Nathan was the one to tell her running away from your problems is sometimes the best option, and she really believed it this time. Kim was running again, but she did not care.

"Hey." His voice was gentle again just like it had been earlier.

"Hey." Nathan was surprised to get a reply from her but took it either way. He decided to go back inside to give her the space she may have needed. But as soon as he sat down on the sofa to watch some TV, Kim was making her way towards him.

Kim sat down on his lap, straddling him. She was being a little too forward for his liking, considering the circumstances. But when she placed her lips on his, Nathan couldn't help but place his hands on her waist and kiss her back. He wanted this to be real, but for some reason, it didn't feel entirely right.

"I'm sorry for overreacting." Kim whispered close to his ear before placing a trail of kisses down his jawline.

It was then, that Nathan stopped what he was doing and pulled back to look her in the eye. He searched her face for signs that this may be a joke but she only went back to kissing him. Her hands found the edges of his jacket and swiftly, she took it off him. Nathan was trembling then, her touch made him freeze although he knew that was a bad idea.

Nathan knew exactly what Kim was doing when her roaming hands found the waistband of his trousers. He was aware of the fact that she was subtly looking for something but did not budge, just held her hips as she kissed his neck and continued on with her search.

Within a matter of seconds, Kim had found his gun and was gripping it tightly in both her hands. She stood up away from Nathan and glared at him whilst pointing the gun in his direction. The cold metal caressed her hands as she gripped it tighter, trying her best to not let her nerves show. The current shock within Nathan diminished by the second until he saw her shaking hands and nervous facial expression- the sight of her was almost laughable.

"Kim, put the gun down." He urged gently.

"Fuck you Nathan. How does it feel now that the tables are turned and I'm the one threatening your life?"

"You know you aren't going to do anything to me Kim so let's cut the bullshit. You really are being ridicu-"

"Don't you dare call me ridiculous you absolute asshole. You dangled me out of that window until I told you I wasn't in control like it was some sick game. You pulled some Blanket Jackson shit on me last night and if you think for a second I'm going to ever forget it you can think again-"

"Kim, you probably still have the safety on."

It took a split second for Kim to point the gun slightly to his left and fire it at a mirror behind him. After the sounds of shattering particles filled the room, Nathan was lost for words. He could tell by the anger in her voice that she had an inability to let go- which was completely understandable. But he wanted her forgiveness, he felt as though he would do anything for it. Nathan also understood Kim was not the type to forgive or forget with time, it troubled him.

"Do you want to bet the goddamn safety is still on?"

A wave of nervous anger fell over her then as she stared into his eyes. Kim felt a lot of things at once then, feelings that reminded her of the times she spent with Shane and it made her feel sick. She knew then that it was probably too late. As she pointed a gun at Nathan's head, she finally realised there was a cocktail of love and hate swirling around inside of her. Kim couldn't decide which was the best to act on just yet.

It took her a moment to set her thoughts straight. All her life she had acted on love- the love she had for her father and his approval, the love she had for her deceiving friends and also the love she had for Shane. This time, she would act on hate. Her mind was made up.

"Give me your wallet." She said.

"Wha-"

"Give me your fucking wallet, I want all the money you have."

"Kim please, just listen to me for a minute."

"I'm done listening to you Nathan. I've had enough of you playing around with me."

"What do you expect to get out of this? You know I'll find you sooner or later."

"Not if I kill you first." She threatened. Kim was quite surprised by the torturous look that fell upon Nathan's face then. Her words felt like they were ripping him apart. He wondered if she had real and true intentions behind all of this or if it was just an act in order to get as far away from there as possible. "Don't give me that look. You threatened my life now I'm threatening yours. Give me your money so I can go."

"Okay, okay." He slowly got up from the sofa to retrieve his wallet and money. Kim followed behind, her aim never leaving him.

She shot at the glass coffee table in an act of pure spite before muttering "Let's see you get the deposit back now."

Nathan savored his last moments with her, although he wished they were spent without the gun and the threats. He took one last look at her that would have to last him for a while.

Nathan noticed the things he had forgotten to take note of earlier- her eyes, her freckled cheeks, her silky hair. He felt the softness of her skin as she practically snatched the wallet from his hands before leaving him alone in the suite by himself.

And just like that, she was gone.

Chapter 22

It took Kim a lot of time to finally get herself back to Portland. After taking Nathan's money, she used it to get multiple buses and buy a disposable phone in order to call one of her friends back in Portland. For a moment or two, she wondered where they thought she had been all this time but remembered then Nathan had suggested before that the CIA would take care of that. They were good at covering things up when needed, he had stated.

Marie, one of the only close friends that Kim remembered a contact number for, picked her up from a bus station in Oregon near Portland. It took only a minute to pass by before Marie spoke. Kim was waiting for her to speak first, in fear that she may tell a different story to the one her friends had been told.

"So... How was Chicago?" Marie eyed her with curiosity. It appeared quite strange to her friend that she would up and leave so abruptly to visit Chicago again- a city Kim had said over and over again that she would never visit again. There was a relief within Kim that Marie couldn't detect once she heard her friend's words next to her.

"Fine."

"That's it? Just fine? You left out of nowhere for weeks and all I get is fine?" There was no doubt that Marie and some of Kim's other friends were concerned about her. She hadn't told them everything about her life back in Chicago but had told them enough for each one to understand Kim was not very comfortable discussing her past.

"I guess it was okay. My father's still an asshole, my brothers are still annoying and my mom is just as bad." Kim supposed it some of what she was saying was in actual fact the truth. Her father hadn't changed at all, considering there were crazy Japanese men trying to hunt her down.

"What about Shane?" Marie was one of the only friends who knew the entire story regarding Shane and Kim's friends.

"I don't know. I didn't see him while I was there."

"All that time and you didn't bump into each other?" What the hell had Kim been doing for all those weeks back in Chicago? Marie wondered.

"Well, I guess I was avoiding him to be honest. I don't want to see him, ever again actually."

Kim wondering why it felt wrong to hold back from talking about Shane then. It was a bizarre feeling for her to process, considering she would almost physically squirm at the mention of his name before her trip. She felt the need to talk about him then, to get everything out of her system but maybe then was not the time. Kim had other things on her mind that needed to be assessed before she focused all of her energy on the question of if she was finally over what Shane had done to her or not.

Shane did not matter to her in that moment- Nathan did. Her journey within him being alongside her was a little more difficult to face than she had ever expected. It felt strange to be without him, probably because they were practically joined at the hip for so long.

There was a gaping hole forming in her being, Kim didn't want to believe it but she knew it was there because of Nathan. The catch up with Marie didn't make her feelings of withdrawal lessen. In fact, the closer she got to her apartment, the worse she felt. Things were going back to normal- as normal as they could be considering the circumstances and the fact that she was still trying to hide from the people after her-and Kim was not warming to the familiar feelings Portland brought her.

Kim's apartment was cleaned up, it was as if Nathan had never broken in and chased her around her kitchen island. The memories were almost laughable had she not been in such a gloomy mood. Marie had sensed it in the car, she knew Kim was not up for talking that day and so left her alone to settle back into her apartment.

Everything looked right, the familiar smell seemed right, but nothing actually felt right to Kim. After spending almost three days traveling, she guessed sleep was all she needed to make herself feel normal again but she had a couple of restless nights before being able to fall into a deep sleep. She had gotten so used to sleeping next to someone that it was difficult for her to adapt to her old surroundings.

Things came in stages regarding Kim's feelings once she arrived back in Portland. The first stage was annoyance. Kim grew angry at small things at first, then it went on to more general and ridiculous things that were not physically possible to change. She would get frustrated at the clouds in the sky and the traffic on the street. She understood that her anger and rage was being directed at the wrong things, and the source of her annoyance was not the everyday things she saw or experienced but actually herself.

She was very angry at herself, and confused by everything she was feeling. Leaving Nathan the way she did felt like both the right and wrong thing to do. Kim felt like she was going crazy from the constant flow of thoughts that would pop into her head about him every few times a day. Kim was angry at herself for caring.

Next came sadness. She truly felt ripped in two, stuck between wanting to see him and never wanting to look at him again. His absence caused a great amount of sorrow to appear in Kim's life that lingered on for a long time after she arrived home. She also worried about what would happen if she was found again, Nathan was not there to protect her anymore.

After sadness, there was only confusion left. Kim understood she cared for him, but knew deep down that caring for a man like him was something she deemed as unacceptable. What had happened to her old attitude of being done with men and relationships? Before Nathan showed up, she was officially washing her hands with romance and everything that came with it. Kim was confused about why she missed Nathan, about why she cared and about why she was feeling all of these things in stages because of his absence.

Kim's friends tried their very best to make her spirits rise again, but it seemed to be no use. They were aware that she was acting different but knew by the way she was acting that she did not want to be questioned.

It took a couple of days for everything to finally sink in and for Kim to settle back into her normal life. The ballet school she worked with quickly got back into contact with her about her job. Ballet was one of the only things she was happy to return to. It was a passion of hers that would not grow old. She put all of her effort into her work instead of focusing solely on Nathan, a man she finally told herself she was done with. Nothing between them would have worked anyway.

Days were spent in and out of the studio, late nights of practising and busy afternoons rehearsing with the younger children in the school. Although things were going back to normal little by little, he was always in the back of her mind. Sometimes people aren't supposed to be constants in one's life, they are only there to take part in it for a little while. Kim guessed that rule applied to Nathan. She had learned from her mistakes. Kim would never involve herself with a man the way she had done without applying and following strict rules. Foolishness and carelessness on both sides were what had ruined their agreement. Both got too caught up in what they were doing, both had cared too much, even just the slightest bit.

There were still some unanswered questions that kept Kim wondering, despite knowing she really should put her thoughts about him to rest. She was in denial about the fact that sleeping next to him would enable her to get the best sleep ever, she was lying to herself about how much she missed his obnoxious voice and their silly bickering, back and forth arguments.

Every night she would make sure his gun was kept in her top drawer beside her bed, along with his empty wallet that allowed her continuous thoughts to wander off. She would get restless every now and then and take both objects out to examine them although it was not necessary.

It was another one of those nights where she was unable to sleep despite having went through a busy day and knowing there was a busier day ahead of her in the morning. Her mind was unable to relax sometimes at night, work was making her mind go into overdrive and she found it difficult to wind down the occasional night.

Kim wanted someone to shake her out of her mood she was in. She didn't need Nathan nor did she want him. She did however, need to snap out of it and forget about him, but it was easier to think about that task rather than actually doing it. Kim couldn't let someone of such little importance in her life cause such a big effect on her attitude towards things in general.

The promise she seemed to be making every time she took out the objects she took from Nathan was being made that night again too. Except tonight was different from the rest, this time she would mean it. The gun was there in case of emergency and that was the only reason she had kept it but his wallet- that was a different story.

The dark leather was cold on her fingertips as she examined it for what felt like the hundredth time since she had arrived back in Portland. This was not kept in case of an emergency, to keep her safe. This was kept as a reminder of him, although she knew it was beginning to sound like she was in a cliché love story, Kim just couldn't help it.

The mystery behind Nathan and his life was still unsolved although with his wallet, she discovered another piece to the puzzle she would most likely never solve. Kim opened the wallet up and looked at the face staring back at her. A face of a stranger that had become familiar to her- the face of a woman she would never know. The small printed picture remained in the same spot it had always been. Kim wanted to leave everything as it was but confusion and complete curiosity irked inside her.

She was prying, she was being too nosey for her own good but despite knowing this, she continued to wonder who the woman might be to Nathan. It certainly didn't look like it would be his mother or a close relation. She looked nothing like him. Her hair hung in red tendrils around her face. She was beautiful, her blue eyes seemed to sparkle in a way Kim couldn't describe. She looked like some sort of model.

It was always in the back of her mind- Stephen's words from the club that night in Las Vegas. Kim just didn't know whether they applied to the woman in this picture and so she tried her best to ignore it. She was unsure as to whether she actually wanted to know who the mysterious woman was in Nathan's wallet or not. Maybe Kim would never know.

She wanted to forget about it then, regretting ever taking the wallet out that night in the first place. But even once she had put the things away and lay down in bed again, her thoughts brought her back to the picture of the woman. Even with her eyes closed shut, she could not erase the worrying thoughts she had. Kim had a bad feeling about that picture- and for all the right reasons.

Chapter 23

It had been two long months since Kim saw Nathan last. Although at first she felt confusion and regret, time had given her the opportunity to forget about him- but not completely. Work made her a very busy woman, she was glad she pursued something she loved or else she would be complaining about how much time work took up in her everyday life.

There was a show everyone in the ballet school were preparing for, one that Kim herself would be performing in along with her class of younger children. This meant her schedule was constantly hectic but she had to admit, she liked the franticness her job brought her. Since stepping back from her situation with Nathan and coming home, she had to admit it felt amazing to work again.

Sometimes though, she had her doubts. Kim was unsure as to whether she was focusing all her energy on this show in order to ensure Nathan didn't creep back into her mind again. There must have been something about him that made him stick in her mind, it confused Kim but she did not want to dwell on the fact. He might remain in her thoughts and come through every now and then, but she wouldn't see him again for a long time at least. He was gone- or so she thought.

It didn't take long once Kim had gotten used to not seeing Nathan, for him to appear again. At first, she doubted herself, she thought her mind was playing tricks on her because of the way in which she would spot him. Nathan's face would pop up every now and then in the strangest of places and from afar. He would never get too close, but remained a certain distance away so that she would be able to acknowledge his presence sometimes.

Kim, strangely enough, didn't feel scared by this. She thought she should be, considering he was most likely following her again to one day take her and bring her to D.C- the reason they even met in the first place. But Nathan never budged. He never tried to even take a step closer to her. If Kim was completely honest, it bugged her a little. Didn't he want to talk? Didn't he want to know what was happening with her?

The answer she felt was the most likely to be true was no. Nathan did not want to know how she was doing, or how work was going. They never had that type of relationship and Kim needed to remember that. Sooner or later, he was going to come for her and bring her back to the CIA- but that idea was so difficult for her to process. This Nathan- the one she wanted- was a fictitious character she had made up during his absence in order to make herself feel better. The reality was that he was like all the other men she had met in her life; hungry for control and power, caring only about themselves. It didn't make sense at all that Kim didn't want to believe those things about Nathan- but she did so anyway.

Kim could avoid the situation with Nathan's random appearances no more when one night, he had the boldness to show up at one of her practises. They were in the theatre late one night getting a last practise in for the day when Kim saw him sitting in one of the farthest seats back. There was little light over the seats on the theatre and so it took her some time to figure out who he was.

Nathan knew it was probably a little too close for comfort but he wanted to make sure she knew he was there that night, and every other night for that matter. He watched carefully as she gracefully danced around the stage. She was beautiful, he thought, but she was also a pain. A pain because she took up too much of his time. She was a nuisance because he became increasingly infatuated with her in such a short time. Kim amazed him, without even doing very much at all. Her company made him feel alive again while her absence made him feel a cocktail of regret and sadness.

Kim obviously chose to ignore his presence at her practised. But after a short while, it was show time and he could not be avoided any longer. Although from her perspective, Nathan didn't mind not being acknowledged, she began to think differently one the first night of her show when his face was staring up at her on the stage just three rows from the front.

She remembered locking eyes with him and wondering what they were both doing. This was all very strange. Surely he should have taken her to D.C by now? Surely people working on her father's side should have also been trying to find her? Kim, yet again, was confused by him. Did she want to have a proper encounter with him or did she want to just be left alone? Kim could not decide.

The last night of the show was when the first encounter in weeks finally happened.

Kim was exhausted and so instead of going out once the show ended, she went straight home. The silence from the apartment filled her ears. She shut her front door and turned on the lights, only to be met by Nathan standing in the kitchen. Kim jumped at the sight of him but then relaxed a little.

"How long have you been standing there in the dark for you creep?" Although she thought it may be best to panic, she felt completely relaxed. It was as if nothing had happened between the two before she returned home.

"Long enough." He spoke after a long pause.

Nathan hadn't saw her face in so long, he was drinking in her features as every minute passed.

"Get out." She forced the words out of her mouth, looking around to try and find the nearest object to throw at him. Nathan was not her friend, he couldn't be. And the only explanation that made sense of why he was here was that he was coming to take her again.

Those two words made him want to do as he was told. Nathan felt ridiculous standing there in her apartment, staring back at her like she was some sort of extra-terrestrial being that he had never laid eyes on before. He felt embarrassed, or as if his pride had been tarnished as he stood there, the reason being, his only motives of showing up there was purely to see her again, to be in such a close proximity that he could reach out and touch her- but he didn't of course.

"No." Nathan finally said.

"I kept your gun, don't think I wont use it-"

"Kim you and I both know you wouldn't shoot me."

"What makes you doubt I'd do that? You aren't very much to me except a pain right now."

"Because you had the perfect opportunity to do it before you left me in Vegas. You care, don't pretend you don't-"

"And I guess I could say the same for you too couldn't I? You've had countless opportunities to shoot me, to just kill me and get your job done easily but you haven't." Kim stared him dead in the eye as she spoke, Nathan knew it was the complete truth but only sighed in response.

Relaxed as ever, she walked over to the kitchen cabinet to find something to eat. Nathan's eyes followed her every move and saw her take out a bag of chips. The noise of the bag being opened sounded strange in the quiet apartment.

"So why are you here then Nathan? We've both established the fact that we haven't killed each other when been given the opportunity to but that doesn't mean a lot. Are you here to finally do your job and take me to D.C?" Kim asked, before eating loudly in front of him.

"I'm not bringing you to D.C. I don't think it's the best idea I already told you. I'm trying to figure things out with the CIA at the minute." He was just short of mumbling to himself.

"So what are you going to do about your job as an agent, they surely can't be okay with you not following through with your mission." Kim didn't want to go to D.C, but didn't understand why he was taking matter into his own hands.

"Well... The CIA don't know anything about this yet."

"So you're basically not following your instructions?"

"You're acting like you want to go?" he shot back in irritation.

"I don't, but I don't see how this is going to work out for you."

"Don't worry about me. I can handle myself fine." Nathan grumbled.

"Good." Kim nodded at him. "So now that I know you're not going to take me again, you can tell me why you're here."

"I-I guess I just wanted to see you."

The eye contact and honesty dripping from his voice was a little too much for Kim to cope with. It caused her to look again and focus on something else in the room. Nathan wanted her to admit she wanted to see him too, but knew well about her stubbornness and inability to forgive. Although she threatened his life like he threatened hers, Nathan was completely willing to forget about that night. He admitted to himself only that Kim could've shot him in the chest multiple times and he would still find forgiving her an easy task to do- that must mean something, but Nathan did not want to wander into that topic right then.

Kim had put the chips down and was standing with her arms crossed then, not knowing what to say until a reminder popped into her head.

"I have something for you." She said awkwardly before leaving the kitchen to find his wallet. Within a minute or so she was back standing in front of his, holding out her hand for him to take it.

Nathan noticed how she couldn't look at him after returning from her bedroom. She felt awkward and nervous, even uncomfortable giving back what belonged to him because of the picture inside. Kim knew he would know exactly what was on her mind but he wasn't a closed book either. The relief that appeared instantly on his face once catching sight of the wallet made her feel guilty for taking it. She knew the picture meant a lot to him, there could be no denying it.

"Thanks."

"Don't mention it." She still couldn't look at him and he felt he should say something. Nathan was aware of the fact that by now, she had seen the picture inside but he wasn't quite sure what she would have thought at the first sight of it. He didn't want her to make assumptions so felt the need to speak again.

"Kim, she's just-"

"It's fine Nathan, you don't need to explain anything to me." Kim understood why he thought an explanation was necessary but it wasn't. She had spent a lot of time wondering who the girl was in the picture, but it was only then when he was standing in front of her that she realised it was none of her business.

"But I just want you to know-"

"Nathan." She finally looked him in the eye and when she did, her stomach leaped at the sight of him. He looked torn apart. "It doesn't matter." Kim forced a small smile but she knew it wouldn't make him feel okay.

"I amn't in a relationship, the entire trip I haven't been and I just wanted you to know that in case you thought otherwise because of the picture." He chose his words carefully.

"Okay." She spoke, her voice barely above a whisper. There was a silence in the room until Kim decided to change the subject. "Where have you been staying?"

"Hotels for the night, sometimes in my car."

"And where are you staying tonight?"

"I don't know yet." She rolled her eyes at his words then before disappearing for another couple of minutes. Nathan waited patiently, wondering what where she had gone, until she came back with sheets and a pillow. He followed her to the sofa where she plopped down the folded sheets and then looked at him when he spoke.

"What are you doing?" he asked.

"Getting you sheets to stay the night. There's no point in you looking for a room somewhere now, it's too late and my couch's better than the driver's seat of your car."

He only nodded them as she lay out the blankets she got for him. It took her some time, giving Nathan the opportunity to take in the sight of her again. She fluffed up the pillow and mumbled something to herself before standing up properly to walk away but Nathan took her wrist before she could go anywhere.

"Thank you." He said gratefully as he looked down at her. He pulled her a little closer in front of him, waiting for her to shrugged out of his grip.

"It's okay, I felt I had to do something considering you're not taking me away yet."

"Kim..." Nathan's eyes focused on her moving lips. His hands had managed to slip around her waist. She was surprised by this and savoured the feel of him being so close again. It had felt like a year since they had been in Vegas but she knew it was nowhere near that long. "I just had to make sure you were okay. I have to keep an eye on you. You never know what's around the corner."

"Let's not talk about that right now." She trailed off, she didn't want to think about who might be coming after her.

Kim wasn't thinking when their lips were just a breath away from each other's. She leaned in just a little closer until she felt his lips skim hers the slightest bit.

"I missed you." She admitted truthfully but knew she was going too far. He was about to kiss her but she then moved her lips away and rested her forehead on his for a moment.

"I missed you too." His words were too real for her to forget. They shared a minute in silence together before she pulled away slowly.

"Goodnight Nathan."

Those were her last words before she disappeared into her room for the night.

Chapter 24

After Kim and Nathan's nearly-kiss, Kim remained very distant and closed off from him, although she had insisted he stay with her instead of in a hotel. It was a week in and Nathan was still sleeping on her couch every night. The pair had become too comfortable with each other, or so Kim thought.

They would share breakfast, she would arrive home from work to dinner with him and they were sit up and watch TV until one, usually Kim, became too tired to keep their eyes open. They lived in harmony together but still Kim remained adamant that they did not share a bed or any close contact. She did not want things to end up too heated between them, because that would cause a relationship like the one they had in Vegas to form.

Kim resisted his touch and every opportunity she had to be physically close to him. It wasn't until one night that Nathan brought up the topic as they shared Chinese take-out and watched some conventional sitcom together. He had reached for her hand only for her to snatch it away quickly.

"Why am I even here Kim?"

"Certainly not to hold my hand anyways Nathan." She retorted before picking at the food she had left behind.

"You're always so guarded."

"I wonder why?" Kim asked sarcastically, although Nathan needed a serious conversation then. "I meant what I said about forgiveness. You get one chance and that's that."

Her words were like stone hitting him in the chest. The time they shared together was definitely not ideal. But Nathan found that during their trip, he had discovered a lot about Kim that not everyone would know. She had opened up to him a couple of times about her life and her feelings and all Nathan wanted right then was to go back to how it had been in those moments when she was nothing but honest, pure and vulnerable.

Did the personal and intimate things they shared between them during their trip not mean anything to her? Nathan felt a great deal of something towards her- but he just hadn't figured out exactly what that something was. It hurt him to see her being so difficult and tough whenever he tried to break down her walls again like he already had a couple of times.

Kim of course, was fighting her instincts and feelings she had towards Nathan. Because she could not let herself be vulnerable or expose herself to any more hurt than she had already faced. The fact that she may have wanted to grab his hand and hold on tight before he had even reached for hers just a minute ago made her feel weak and helpless when it came to Nathan. She had to keep this façade going, she had to look out for herself and no one else.

The movement of Nathan beside her on the sofa snapped her out of her daze then. She was quite surprised to see him stand up and make his way to the door where his coat was hanging up. Kim followed along behind him like a lost puppy and stood beside the door, looking at him with confusion etched onto her features.

"Where are you going?" she asked, sounding a little too concerned for her liking.

"Maybe it's better if I don't stay here anymore. I should go-"

"No."

"No?" he asked, unsure what she had meant.

"Don't go." Kim looked up at him, her eyes pleading with him more than her words. Nathan let out a deep sigh, unable to comprehend what was going on. There was a short pause before he spoke.

"Kim, we're living in this constant flow of nothingness. I see you every day, we talk and interact but nothing is actually happening."

"What exactly did you want to happen? Did you only come back here so you could try to get me in bed again?" Kim narrowed her eyes at him, completely misunderstanding his words.

"Of course not!" he exclaimed. "You know I didn't mean that."

"Well that's what it sounded like."

"I know you don't want me like that anymore." His voice was quieter then, he took both her hands between his and held them tight before looking directly at her before he explained. "I'm not talking about sex Kim, I'm talking about actual conversations, about sharing things with one another. I want you to walk through the door and tell me everything about your day and what pissed you off. I want all the interesting stuff and the boring stuff too. You just don't seem to care and whatever emotional thing we had growing between us is clearly gone although I wish it wasn't. I can tell you don't want me to be here and I understand why, so it's better if I just leave."

"But I don't want you to leave." Her words were full of meaning and truth, they were the most honest thing she had uttered to Nathan since her confession that she missed him.

"I find that very hard to believe. Maybe I should just start accepting the fact that things won't be the same again. What we had was fucked up from the beginning and I don't know if it would even be possible to have something with you, but I was willing to give it a try. Now I'm not quite sure..." As he finished his sentence he let go of her hands and it was then that Kim began to panic a little.

"I just- it's hard to explain." Kim couldn't believe she was going to beg him to stay. Only a moment ago she was keeping to her promise that she would stay as distant as possible with him. "I don't know what I should be doing with my life and I'm still wary. I want you here but I don't know why. I feel like forgiveness is the one thing that can make us okay again but it's difficult for me Nathan."

"Well then why not just forget? Why can't we both just forget about that night? Forget about everything that happened on that trip and start over." His words caused a pained expression to appear on her face. She wanted to admit that forgetting was something she just could not do, but she also wanted things to be okay again. If she tried to forget, she felt like she would be willingly leaving herself prone to getting hurt again.

In a short moment, he opened the front door and that brought Kim's decision making to a halt. She done what she felt right and grabbed his arm. Nathan looked at her in surprise.

"I don't know if I can forget about everything right now. I'm unsure about everything between us. But what I definitely am sure about, is that I don't want you to go. I want you to stay here with me. And maybe that means something? Maybe I could try to forget, if you'll do the same."

Kim thought it should feel like she was making the wrong decision, but it didn't. The feeling should scare her a little but she only brushed it off, still waiting on his next move. Nathan was staring at her, he was quite shocked from her honesty and her reaction altogether.

"Of course I would do the same Kim. I like you, I really do and I want us to work out, not in the same way as Vegas." Kim gulped, she felt the same but didn't know whether to admit that or not. Nathan noticed how she looked like she was about to say something. Her undecidedness shone through in her features and so he took a step towards her and leaned closer to her face, one of his hands in her hair. Kim was avoiding eye contact for a moment, but then looked at him and spoke.

"I feel the same way; I want to try." Kim's voice was quiet and gentle. Her words brought relief to Nathan. He took a step away from her then to close the door and looked at her then.

It took only a moment before he reached out and took her close in his arms for a tight hug. It was the closest contact they had since the night they nearly kissed a while ago but this time, Kim wasn't trying to hold herself back. She savoured every second but decided she needed to tell him how she was feeling. Kim pulled away and looked at him.

"We need to take things slow, we don't know what's around the corner or what's going to happen."

"I completely agree with you." Nathan nodded, under-standing what she had said but only an hour later Kim was in bed when she heard him knocking on her door.

She was contemplating whether to get up out of bed and answer when just moment later, the door creaked open. Nathan stuck his head through the open door to check whether she was asleep yet. Should she pretend to already have fallen asleep? She would feel terrible if she did, and it was so tempting to just tell him to come in. She needed to make up her mind.

"Kim?" he whispered. There was a moment of silence be-fore she finally answered.

"Yes?"

"Can I sleep in here tonight?"

"Okay, as long as you stick to your side of the bed." Kim didn't want to sound happy with the fact that they were going to share a bed but she was.

"I will. I promise."

Chapter 25

"I will. I promise." After he spoke, she felt the bed dip down as he got in beside her.

"Goodnight Nathan." Kim was transported back to the time they spent on their trip when they would share a bed every night. "Where are the handcuffs eh?" they both chuckled and then Nathan turned over on his side to look at her.

"Goodnight Kim." His voice was gentle, it made her want to say something else but she didn't know whether pillow talk was appropriate considering the circumstances. Wasn't she supposed to be the one who didn't want him anymore?

"Nathan?" she said after a moment or two of looking up at the ceiling above her bed. Kim could feel his eyes on her the entire time, she knew he hadn't turned from his spot on his side.

"Mhm?" he replied, curious as to what she was going to say next.

"Remember the night we went to the casino with Stephen and Felicity?"

"Yes." Nathan didn't quite know whether he wanted to hear what she had to say just then.

"Why were you being like that with her?" she too turned on her side then so that she was looking at him, or a version of his, his figure distorted from the lack of light in the room. Her eyes had adjusted to the darkness in the room and she almost thought she could see a painful expression form on his face.

"I-I don't know."

"Please." Kim scoffed at him before adding, "You must have a reason. I guess there was no rules against what you two were doing with each other but I'm just curious. I just really want to know."

"I guess I wanted to make you jealous."

"Well I knew you wanted a reaction out of me, but why? Why would you want to make me jealous? I don't understand. I didn't do anything wrong did I?"

"No, of course you didn't. I was just being stupid. I should've never done it."

"Did she really kiss you first? You don't have to lie to me Nathan, that would make me even more disappointed- I know I shouldn't have been disappointed in the first place but-"

"Kim, you should have been disappointed. It's understandable, sometimes sex draws you in, but then you start to learn more about the person and you end up- nothing never mind. If I had've seen you doing the same thing I would've been disappointed too. But she was the one to kiss me. I didn't kiss her."

Kim suddenly felt foolish, even if Felicity was the initiator, it was still Nathan's fault. She shouldn't justify what he had done.

"You still made her feel like you would've kissed her back so I guess it doesn't really make a difference." There was a short pause before he spoke.

"I'm sorry Kim. I really am. I know sorry might mean nothing to you right now but I just want you to know that I regret that entire night. I would never have let you fall out of that window, I just needed some sort of validation of control. But instead it only made me realise something else. I know sorry doesn't mean much but I just want you to know how I'm feeling."

"Okay." She almost whispered while nodding at him.

He wanted to reach out and take her into his arms, needing the closeness again but he knew he couldn't. She wanted to take things slow and if that was what she needed, he would obey her wants.

"I'm sorry too."

"For what?" he furrowed his brows at her.

"For what I done afterwards with Stephen, I hope you know it was only me involved in my actions. Stephen would never have agreed but I forced him. I was angry and I wanted you to know how I had been feeling all night."

"I guess it's my fault then."

"Tell Stephen I'm sorry too, I hope you weren't angry at him. He seems like a good friend to you. He really does care about you Nathan. And real friends are hard to find." The last sentence was laced with some sort of emotion Nathan was trying to figure out although Kim hoped he hadn't picked up on it.

"Kim..." Nathan was a little worried. She had turned again to lie on her back then, not able to look at him for a moment. She knew what he was thinking, but he was unsure whether to ask or not. Ever since the beginning Nathan wanted to know the full story of what happened between Kim and her friends before she moved away from Chicago.

"Shane cheated on me with one of my friends." Kim had finally said it, although she felt truly humiliated from the confession. "That's what happened, after I found out about my father, I began to open my eyes and look around at every part of my life although I didn't want to see what other lies I would discover."

"I'm sorry." It pained him to hear her talk the way she had, to hear that raw emotion come out in her words.

"It was going on for a while too, it wasn't just a once off. And all my friends knew about it and never told. I know you might think I'm a little too cautious, and too unforgiving but I just don't want people to hurt me like that again. I just- I just let them. I was so stupid that I never even figured it out."

"It wasn't your fault Kim, you didn't just let them do it. They were going to do it either way. Don't blame yourself for other people's wrongdoings." His words were a desperate plea for her to not feel the way she did, but it would probably do very little for Kim. After she did not reply, Nathan spoke again. "God, I'm such a fucking asshole. I shouldn't have said those things that night in Vegas, I don't know why I did." He sat up a little so he could see her face. It was then that he discovered she was crying. He reached out and wiped a couple of tears away.

"It's fine."

"It's not fine."

"I feel better now that I'm telling someone about it. It feels like a weight lifted off my shoulders, so thank you for listening. Don't beat yourself up too much about what you said, you weren't the only one who said things they regret. I do feel a little better now, honestly." She had stopped crying by then and turned her head to the right to look at Nathan who wasn't fully convinced.

"It feels good to just say it. To just admit that I fucked up with my judgement of my friends and Shane. I'm over him, but getting over what he done is a little more difficult." Kim added before yawning.

Again, a silence fell upon them, it was filled with something Kim could not explain. Nathan was holding back; she could sense it but said nothing. If he had anything to say, she would not force him to say it.

"Her name was Madison... the girl in the wallet." Was being the word that Kim zoned in on, she realised she did not want Nathan to say something he was not comfortable saying.

"Just because I've told you pretty much everything now doesn't mean you have to open up to me too Nathan. I get it if you don't want to talk about it."

"No, I do Kim."

"I just don't want you to feel forced into telling me things you don't want to tell me. I understand." Kim said.

"I want to tell you." He admitted. "Her name was Madison and she was my girlfriend for a very long time." Although the words brought him agony, he fought through them.

"What happened to her Nathan?" Kim could already tell where this was going. She heard him gulp loudly before speaking again.

"Kevin Green. He had her killed. He didn't stop after taking away my mother and father, he kept on going and decided to take away Madison too." She had never heard him speak like he had then, his voice full of suffering and anguish.

"Nathan-"

"Please don't feel sorry for me. I told you already I don't want you to feel sorry for me. I have to live with the pain and no amount of revenge will ever bring her or my parents back. I learned that the hard way, vengeance doesn't make you feel any better."

"How long were you two together?"

"A couple of years, since we were teenagers. She helped me deal with my parents passing away. She was with me through all of the pain I felt after they died, for the months and years that followed and I messed up."

"What do you mean you messed up Nathan?" Kim didn't understand.

"I mean we shouldn't have been together, the people I love are punished because of me and that's not fair. I should have never let her in, because if I didn't she would still be here today."

Kim told him how it wasn't his fault, he needed to forgive himself in order to let go. Nathan told her all about Madison, how he loved her and what she was like. It didn't feel strange to hear about another woman, Kim even felt like she wanted to know more. Maybe it was because the more he talked, the more he seemed to be at ease with himself. It was one of the few times Nathan seemed vulnerable in Kim's eyes.

Although Madison was on Nathan's mind that night, something else was bothering him too, something that involved Kim. She was unaware of it, but he knew people from her father's side were coming and it wouldn't take them long to get there. Nathan had no proof of this but found it strange that no one had tried to take Kim away again.

His boss was looking for him too and he knew exactly where to find him. There was no hiding, but Nathan needed time to think things through and come up with a plan but he had little time then. There was only so many times he could ignore his boss's calls before he would come and find Nathan himself. He had to make up his mind- sooner rather than later.

What was he supposed to do with Kim? He didn't want her to go away, she was innocent and neither side valued her life. He felt stuck and unsure but Kim noticed this and turned to look at him again, confusing his anxiety with discomfort from the topic they had previously been talking about.

Nathan's mind ran from one subject to another. Madison then Kim and back to Madison. This was his opportunity to let it all go, to tell Kim everything. Not because she wanted to know but because he wanted to tell her.

Nathan opened to Kim about everything that night. He did not just tell her what happened, between the death of his parents and Madison's also, he explained to her how it felt to go through those tragedies. Kim could feel his pain and despair through his words. The raw emotions he was allowing to be seen by her were too much in moments when he described what it was like to wake up every morning and realise his parents were not there anymore, that the love of his life also was gone.

And after everything, all the memories and feelings he passed on to her, she understood him. Even if it was only for a moment or two, she felt something indescribable for him. It disappeared as quickly as it had come to life, but it still lingered- it would for a long time. When he was finished speaking, he felt this sort of freedom, this escape he found in Kim. He was not running away anymore; he was facing what had happened with someone new.

In the end, Kim did not explain how sorry she was for his loss, she did not want him to think she felt sorry for him. Instead of using any words, she acted instead. Kim reached out her hand and grabbed his tightly in hers. The space remained between them, as they both stared up at the ceiling above them instead of at each other. To Nathan, it felt like the night he had gotten shot when she held his hand through the pain. Back then, her touch was too intense for him but now, it was what he needed. He did not pull away like last time, instead he squeezed her hand tighter.

Chapter 26

"**S**he isn't going to be safe forever Nathan. You know she'd be better off with us than with her father's associates. And believe me when I say they are coming, it's only going to be a matter of days."

His boss's words of persuasion were enough to make his core shake. He didn't know what to do in the situation he had planted himself into. Nathan knew for sure it would only be a matter of time before the CIA got in contact with him, but he had been too busy spending his time with Kim to realise that it was going by quicker than he expected.

"I need time to think."

"You don't have any time left. If you won't bring her in, I'll find someone to do the job for me instead."

"Just give me one more day okay? If you bring anyone near her I swear to god, we'll be gone and you'll end up having to try and find us."

"Is that a threat Nathan?"

"Look, I just need another day or two to wrap my head around everything okay? I won't keep you waiting."

"The only reason I'm even entertaining your behaviour is because you're the best at your job-usually. Don't let me down Nathan."

Nathan said his goodbyes and then hung up the phone before taking a deep breath. He didn't know what he was going to do. Would running work? It was a silly option to think about, considering they would be found quickly, running would only prolong the anticipation. Maybe Kim was better off in the CIA's hands? Nathan wasn't convinced. He would put it all to the back of his mind for now, he didn't want Kim worrying.

He made his way back into Kim's apartment building and upstairs. When he opened the door and found Kim exactly where he had left her, cooking them both dinner, he tried his best to give her a reassuring smile although he knew she was more than a little sceptical.

"Why were you gone for so long?" although there was little force in her voice, Nathan could tell she felt like something was wrong.

"I was just talking on the phone."

"To who?" Kim wished she didn't feel the need to question him, but she did. She was suspicious and she hated it.

"Just to Stephen, we haven't talked in a while. Kim you don't have anything to worry about okay?" He lied to her because he felt like it was the best thing to do for her.

"Okay." She said quietly. By then he had made his way over to stand behind her in the kitchen. She was chopping vegetables when he wrapped his arms gently around her and planted a soft kiss on her cheek.

"Do you need any help?" he spoke into her neck before kissing it.

"I'm good thanks." Kim whispered, focusing on his kisses. She turned her head slightly then and before she could say anything else, he captured her lips for a long, heated kiss. His touch made her shiver but she pulled away after a moment.

"We're supposed to be taking things slow Nathan." Her voice was quiet and almost painful. It had been about a week since the night they shared her bed together but Kim was still adamant on holding back from anything physical except for the occasional peck he would give her. She knew what she wanted and it was becoming more and more difficult to refrain from doing anything.

"I know, I know. Forget it, I'm sorry." He felt guilty then for putting her in this position but he couldn't help the want he had to be closest to her. He rested his chin on her shoulder, waiting for her to reply but when she hesitated further he stood up straight and walked into the living room area. "If you need me for anything let me know." He called before sitting down on the sofa in front of the TV.

An hour or so later, they ate dinner and were cuddled up watching some documentary when there was a knock at the door. It startled the two of them although Nathan refrained from allowing his emotions to come through in his exterior. The pair looked at each other before Kim got up from the sofa to answer it. But Nathan grabbed her hand to stop her from doing so, he didn't know what would be on the other side of that door but he had a feeling it wouldn't be good.

"You wait here while I get it." Nathan stood up then and walked quietly over to the door. Kim watched with anticipation, her nerves were driving her up the wall as she waited to find out what would happen next.

It took him a minute to compose himself and finally open the door. And when he was met with a tall, blonde haired woman standing in front of him.

"Who the hell are you?" she asked. Kim thought her voice sounded familiar and walked over to the door to see who it was.

"Marie?" Kim asked once she stood at the door beside Nathan.

"Yes, do you remember your friend Marie? The one you haven't been out with in forever." Marie looked Nathan up and down before stepping inside. Nathan let out a sigh of relief after discovering Kim knew this girl.

"I've been busy, I'm sorry."

"Busy eh?" Marie scoffed before looking at Nathan again, "I guess he's a good enough excuse."

"Marie..." Kim blushed a little and noticed Nathan was grinning at her.

"Hello, I'm Marie. And who might you be?" Marie held out her hand for Nathan to shake.

"This is Nathan." Kim stepped in before he could open his mouth before shooting him a knowing look.

"I'm sure he can speak for himself Kim, not to worry."

"I'm afraid he can't. He was just going actually, weren't you Nathan?" Kim gulped, her eyes almost pleading with him silently. He wasn't quite sure what to say, both women stood staring at him waiting for his reply.

"You know Kim you sound awful suspicious." Marie squinted at her friend before scanning over the apartment. "You two look like you were settled in for the night?"

She only let out a nervous laugh in response to her friend's conclusion. Marie began to make herself at home.

"I was thinking we could go out tonight?" Marie said from the sofa she sat down on.

"I'm not sure..."

"C'mon Kim, what's happening to you? Ever since that trip back to Chicago you haven't been the same." Nathan looked at Kim quizzically, wondering how she was going to get the two of them out of this situation they called Marie. "Nathan can come too." Marie felt the need to add, in case Kim was only hesitant because she didn't want to lose out on time with him. Marie would not blame her.

"He-"

"Of course, I'd love that. It would be fun." Nathan cut across Kim before she could decline the offer before sending her a smug smile. She only narrowed her eyes at him in response.

"Great! Maybe you two should go and get ready. Don't keep me waiting." Marie joked and turned her attention then to the TV.

She could not see Kim grab Nathan by the arm and lead him into her bedroom. Kim shut the door behind them and glared at Nathan, fury burning in her eyes. All he done in response was laugh.

"What the hell was that?" she asked, crossing her arms then.

"What?"

"Nathan I swear to god-"

"Maybe we should go out. It would be a good idea."

"No, it wouldn't. I want you to go back out there and tell Marie that you can't go tonight."

"So you want to go and leave me here on my own?" a taunting, wicked smile crossed his lips which made her angrier.

"No, I don't want to go in the first place and especially not with you." Her words made his smile falter a little, she noticed this but was too annoyed to care then.

"Kim, go and get ready. We're going out. Besides, I want to meet your friend." It had been a while since he had been this playful and arrogant with her, right then, she definitely did not miss it.

"No." she huffed.

"Fine then, I'll go on my own. Maybe Marie will have some things to share with me about you-"

"Oh forget it." Kim stomped off into her bathroom and shut the door. How dare he dictate what she done. She did not want him to meet her friends but used her fear that their stories would not add up as an excuse for this when in actual fact, she was afraid that would be crossing the line too much. Sure, Kim wanted to share more with him, they already had felt more exposed around each other than with anyone else before. But that did not mean she would immediately let him in on all aspects of her life. She did not want that, she wanted to take things slow, very slow.

Kim mulled over the previous events as she entered her shower and turned on the water. She faced the wall and let the water cascade down her body. It took only two minutes before she heard Nathan enter the bathroom, she assumed he was getting himself ready too but then suddenly she felt his presence behind her in the shower. Kim wanted to turn around and face him but she didn't, afraid she would do something she shouldn't.

"Nathan..." she warned him quietly.

"Do you want me to leave?" he had not touched her yet, he needed her to answer his question first.

"I don't know." Kim hesitated although she knew the answer was no. "This is ridiculous, what are you even doing in here? We need to get ready-"

"Shh Sweetheart." He whispered in her ear then. "I'm just here to help. I won't try anything, I promise." Kim wondered why she wanted him so badly to break that promise but shook off the thought. Where had this playful side of Nathan appeared from again? It felt strange to her to see him this way again but without realising, she welcomed him back with open arms.

Within a second, he was lathering soap on her back and pretending as if the call from his boss earlier had never happened.

Chapter 27

"**W**hat am I doing here?" Nathan groaned to himself.

"You're the one who wanted to come?" Kim snorted as she danced around him.

"Biggest mistake ever." He rolled his eyes. Talking over the loud music was becoming irritating.

"Aw... Why? Don't you like dancing?" Kim called as she moved around him to stand in front of him, still moving her hips to the music. "You need another drink. Here, have mine." She practically shoved the drink down his neck. He did not say no, she was too drunk for him to refuse without her causing a fuss so instead, he gulped back the double vodka and coke.

"Kim..." Nathan warned her as she wrapped her hands around his neck and moved to the music. She was too close for comfort, considering a couple of hours ago she would not even kiss him.

"What?" she whispered in his ear as she placed one hand on his jawline. "You need to loosen up." She giggled although it was not just the alcohol making her feel this way, she felt some sort of happiness she hadn't felt in quite some time as she looked into his eyes then.

"Let's go back to the table." He took her hand and lead the way back to where Kim's friend Marie was sitting talking to someone. Along with Marie, a couple more friends arrived at the club a little later in the night.

On their arrival, Nathan noticed Kim looked uncomfortable although she tried to hide it. After introducing them all to Nathan, Kim took Marie off to the side to talk to her while he stayed there.

"Marie?" Kim narrowed her eyes at her friend.

"What?" Marie acted oblivious.

"You said it was just going to be us."

"Why does it matter? They are our friends... The more the merrier."

"Because- because Nathan is here too. I don't want to overwhelm him with this amount of new people."

"He seems fine to me." Marie nodded in his direction, causing Kim to look over at the table and spot her friends and Nathan laughing at something. It was as if the scene was perfectly timed. "Kim, by the looks of it, whatever it is you two have going on, it's been going on a while. You're going to have to let him in sometime. We're your friends, and he's going to have to meet us all someday anyways- it he gets that far."

Marie knew Kim was apprehensive when it came to love. She did not blame her, considering her circumstances and what her ex-fiancé had done to her a couple years ago.

"How come never mentioned him?" She asked.

"I didn't think he was worth mentioning." Kim tried to play it off.

"Oh c'mon." the other woman scoffed, "Of course he's worth mentioning. He's absolutely gorgeous, he's funny and you two seem to get along well."

"We've only started seeing each other." They had hadn't they? Kim wasn't sure when their actual relationship began or whether it had even happened yet? She was confused, one part of her wanted an actual relationship while the other told her not to trust him. It was a constant battle with herself- trying to keep away from him yet wanting to be as close as possible.

Why couldn't it be simple, straight forward, easy? Her sub- conscious sent her a reminder again that whatever type of relationship both she and Nathan shared, it was not going to last long. It simply couldn't. So why was she holding back?

She remembered the night Nathan had opened up to her about Madison and felt an aching in her chest for him. She cared. A lot. And it was scaring her to a point that instead of thinking clearly, she increased her consumption of alcohol after they got back to the table where Nathan and the rest were situated.

Kim's mind was racing, every drink making her feel worse. She was confused, her memories involving Nathan jumbled uncontrollably in her mind. Could she really trust him? She did not want to think about the answer to that spontaneous question that night. She remembered the feel of his touch, the countless games of eye spy he refused to play and the day he held her as she cried uncontrollably about how much of a mess her lie had become. For tonight anyway... her answer to the question would be yes.

"Hey, maybe you should slow down a little Sweetheart. I don't want you getting too drunk on me." He spoke with humour in his voice but he was concerned for her also.

"The only way you're going to get me to stop drinking is to take me home." Kim felt more than a little tipsy then. She giggled and looked at him with eyes full of lust. Nathan knew this was a bad sign- not for himself but for Kim. She did not want anything to happen yet between them and he was respecting her wishes, but drunk Kim had a completely different view than the sober one.

"C'mon then, let's get you home."

She held onto his arm as he ushered her out of club after saying their goodbyes to her friend. It took no time to find a cab home and within a couple minutes, Nathan was locking Kim's front door behind them.

"Let's go to bed." She said suggestively, dragging his arm as she walked in the direction of her room.

"Um, maybe I should sleep on the couch tonight. You go get settled in. I'll be fine out here." He insisted although it pained him to say it.

"You aren't sleeping on the couch." Her words were slurred slightly as she tried to keep her balance and drag him with her.

After many minutes of objecting, Nathan finally gave in. They quickly got ready for bed and it didn't take Kim long before she pulled him closer and planted her lips on his for an eager kiss. Nathan ignored the guilt he felt, in that moment he just kissed her again. She moved from his lips to his jawline to his throat where she rested her head for a moment, inhaling his scent. It was then that she tugged at the hem of his t-shirt in bed and straddled him.

"Kim..." Nathan's voice was a warning for both himself and Kim. She did not want this, he knew if she were not so drunk, she would have said goodnight and sent him to bed on the sofa as soon as they returned home.

"What?" she asked before going back to what she was doing.

"We can't do this."

"Why?" Her expression showed her evident disappointment.

"Because as much as I want to, I know the feeling isn't mutual."

"How much more mutual can this get?" Kim looked down between them then back up to Nathan's pained face.

"You're drunk. Just go to sleep."

"But I don't want to." She groaned as he put her down beside him in bed again.

"You'll thank me in the morning." He whispered in her ear before kissing her forehead. The two turned in bed to look at one another.

"I was right that day in the car about you being a stick in the mud." Kim allowed the words to drunkenly tumble out of her mouth, to which Nathan replied with a loud and echoing laugh that surrounded them both in the room.

"Maybe you were, yes." She blinked at him, taking in his perfect features. Right then, Kim felt like she hadn't been appreciating him up until that moment. Why were her thoughts going from one extreme to another tonight?

"Can we play eye spy again?" her question earned another chuckle from Nathan.

"Tomorrow. Now, sleep."

"Okay." She yawned.

"Are you sure about this?"

"Most definitely."

"If you're not telling the truth Nathan, I swear to-"

"I am. I know exactly where she is and when she will be there. No more playing around. I'm finishing what I started."

"What made you change your mind?" his boss was quizzical then. "It's obvious you've developed some sort of attachment to this girl by now."

"Nothing I can't break off easily."

Chapter 28

"I wish that we could stay like this forever." Kim said her thoughts aloud. She was being completely honest with both herself and Nathan- finally.

They were lying on the sofa in her apartment. There was not a sound in the room after she spoke. There were no distractions, it was just the two of them. Nathan had his arms around her loosely, enjoying the warmth her body gave him. The smell of her sweet perfume engulfed him, so did her words. They made him forget everything else.

"So do I." he admitted.

Kim turned in his arms and looked up at him, propping her head up with her arm. She played with his shirt for another minute or two before speaking again.

"I wish a lot of things were different about all of this, I wish I was different. But I can't be, because I know what's coming for us." It felt right to voice her concerns with him then, he was a soothing presence.

"Shh, don't think like that." He said, although her thoughts were justified if she had have known about his conversation with his boss. He couldn't tell her, but didn't know what he was going to do but telling her was not an option. She would not understand and run.

"I feel right with you... It's very- strange." Kim's intuition had spoken up within her, she felt like this was the calm before the storm. Maybe not tomorrow or the next day, but soon, sometime, things would change. She might never get the chance to say how she felt if she continued to keep it inside.

"Strange huh?" he chuckled at her words.

"Yeah, it's hard to explain. But I've never gotten the chance to open up completely to anyone before, mostly because I've never really given anyone a chance. With you it just happened."

He wished her honesty would make him feel joy, but instead it only intensified his guilt. Through all of it he had to pretend that everything was fine, that he was fine.

"And I can say the same about you too." Nathan spoke softly before placing a kiss on her forehead to which she snuggled closer to him and closed her eyes.

"Remember I jumped off the balcony into that pool to get away from you?" Kim giggled, feeling nostalgic then.

"Are you seriously asking me do I remember it? How could I forget. I had to run back out after you." He joined in then with the laughter and played with her hair.

"You were such a stick in the mud."

"And you were such a brat. You still are." He teased her. "How come I haven't seen you in those care bear pyjamas since our road trip?" Nathan smirked at her.

"Oh shut it you. I burned those as soon as I got back here. I had enough of all your joking around about them."

"They were the definition of sexy." Nathan said sarcastically causing a burst of laughter to erupt from Kim's chest.

She felt like telling him then, exactly how she felt- but something was holding her back. More than one thing actually. Maybe she was afraid. Afraid of the rejection she might receive in return for her complete honesty. She was terrified that Nathan would not feel the same or that he was like all the others that had let her down in more ways than one. It was petrifying to feel something so intense towards another person, without having any particular, solid reason to. And without knowing if the things you felt were only one-sided or not. Kim's apprehension was entirely justified.

But what was she supposed to do with all the things she was feeling kept inside? It was difficult to decide where she and Nathan were going because they did not know what or who was around the corner.

Shane was someone she once loved but did not love enough, at the right time in her life. She had a great job, a stable life, plenty of money for the wedding they were planning to have and surrounded by friends and family. Everything around her crumbled and she was left alone. And then, Nathan came along. He was not supposed to be the one she revealed her true self to. In fact, he was not supposed to be anything to her- but he was and there was no going back. Kim felt everything at once for Nathan, but it was at the wrong time.

"Thank you, Nathan." She felt the urge to say it.

"Jeez, what's gotten into you Kimmy Kim? You're being so nice to me. For some reason, I feel like this is a trap?" Nathan grinned at her then, before noticing how serious her facial expression had become. "What are you thanking me for exactly?" he needed to know, he was confused by her thank you.

"For being here when I needed to let the past spill out of me. I've been holding it in for a while now. I've told others about my version of everything that's happened but not the one I've told you. And thank you for sharing your past with me too."

"Forget about the past now, you need to live your life for now and tomorrow, not what happened yesterday."

He made her feel like everything that happened before him didn't matter. The past only made her who she was if she allowed it to be that way- Nathan had thought her that and it meant a lot to her now that she was looking back on everything.

"You should've been a motivational speaker instead of a CIA Agent Nathan." Kim said dryly, going back to her old self within a matter of seconds. It made Nathan feel a little more comfortable then- because of what he had done to her, he did not want Kim to be nice to him. He didn't deserve it.

It was nice to see her like this for just one last time, both of them getting along and having a good time together without doing very much at all. Tomorrow, things would be different, but he hoped she would soon learn why he chose to do what he did. Of course, not instantly, it would take Kim some time, but one day she would.

"Maybe I should have Kim." Nathan spoke before sighing. He would miss her. But knowing she would be alive and safe rather than staying with her for longer while her life was in danger because of her father. Those business associates of his were dangerous, if and when they got hold of her, there would be no holding back. He saw it with his own eyes before when they were chased out of their hotel room. The only thing that surprised him about this whole situation in Kim's life was the fact that they had not come to get her yet, it was scary to imagine that happening. At least if the CIA were involved and took her, there was a chance of things finally being sorted out. She deserved the best, and her life back, sadly Nathan could not be the person to give her those things, but the CIA were the closest to making her life go back to normal. At least, that was what he hoped for...

"Maybe I should get up and make us something to eat. Are you hungry yet?"

"I'm starving." He yawned before stretching out next to her.

Kim leaned in to kiss him on the lips before attempting to get up off the sofa but he pulled her back and captured her lips once more before speaking.

"Why don't I organise dinner tonight huh?"

"Are you sure you won't give me food poisoning?" Kim looked at him suspiciously before he chuckled and got up.

"You'll have to just wait and see I suppose." Nathan gave her a sly smile before heading off into her kitchen. She turned on the sofa so that she could get a clear view of him.

Maybe her initial intuition was false, because looking at him right then, Kim didn't feel like she had anything to worry about.

Epilogue

The time had finally come, it was the day that everything would change for Kim- and she didn't even know yet.

They talked over the dinner Nathan made and shared the same bed the night before. Kim wasn't afraid of the close contact anymore and fell comfortably into a deep sleep in his arms. Everything was beginning to mend itself between Nathan and Kim at that time- she knew the change would remain gradual. But that was only until she heard the noise of her front door being put through.

Nathan had gone to the bathroom as soon as he woke up which left her in her bed alone. After the loud noise from outside, the apartment went quite but not for long. Kim got out of bed quietly but quickly. She crept over to her door and opened it slowly, only to be grabbed unexpectedly by a tall man dressed in dark clothes.

Kim tried frantically to get loose from the tight grip the man had on her. She kicked and scratched but it was no good.

"Nathan! Help!" she screamed but then a hand went to cover her mouth. She bit down hard on it to try and get free but the man was not moving it any time soon. Kim struggled for breath until the man shoved her against the wall and uncovered her mouth.

Kim was shocked when she had a moment to look around to find that there was not just one man, but a huge group. A second later Nathan appeared, looking absolutely appalled. This was it, she thought, this was the moment she was surprised although she shouldn't have been. It was expected that the men that worked alongside her father would find her sooner rather than later.

She kicked the man who pinned her to the wall, daring him to make his next move which was a rough shove. Kim hit her head off the wall behind her and winced with the pain.

"Hey! Don't hurt her." Nathan demanded loudly but seemed much calmer to Kim than all of the other times they had come across people who worked with her father.

"The bitch kicked me."

It was when she heard his American accent, that Kim noticed this man was not Japanese like the others she had come across during her and Nathan's trip. Her eyes quickly scanned the room to discover none of the men were. She was confused when Nathan looked as composed as ever, the penny still had not dropped when he looked at her with sad eyes.

"Kim Scott, you're under arrest." One of the men who was not surrounding her said. It was then she realised these men did not work for her father, they worked for the government.

"W-What? Why?" she exclaimed angrily, although she got no reply. The man who had grabbed her at first attempted to move her out of the apartment without much force but it was no use, Kim was not budging.

It took three or four men to grab her and drag her from her rooted spot. It took them much longer as she made it extremely difficult, struggling against their great force. Kim didn't know who to be angrier with, the men for being so rough or Nathan for doing nothing at all. He only watched with a grim look on his face. They almost had her out the door when she shouted again.

"Nathan! Do something?"

"You think he's going to help you now Kim? He's the one who turned you in." The man who announced her arrest said in a bitter tone. Kim stopped moving, her entire body went limp when the man's words filled her eyes. The men found it easier to take her away then, as she was completely frozen.

A million things ran through her mind. She would have allowed her expectant tears to fall if her apartment was not full but she needed to keep a strong and tough exterior, just like the one she had when she first met Nathan. The one that fizzled out through weeks and months of his company. Oh, how she had been so foolish to allow that to happen, to allow herself to like him despite their circumstances.

"Kim, I can explain-"

"Not right now you can't. We're taking her to DC immediately, something you should've done a long time ago."

"God damn it Nathan why are you such an asshole?!"

"Kim-" Nathan begged her as she was being taken away, he followed behind as he spoke.

"I can't fucking believe you, you know that? I should have never trusted you!"

Kim shouted loudly in a rage, despite knowing her neighbours would hear. How could Nathan turn her in? She couldn't understand, she would never understand. She had fallen for a man who did nothing but betray her and there was nothing she could do about it. All she could feel was this heaviness on her chest, this complete and total regret but there was no going back.

All of the nights they shared together, all of the jokes and I-Spys, everything had meant nothing to him yet it meant a great deal to her. Kim had been fucked over too many times, by people she never imagined would be capable of betraying her so why had she been so surprised by Nathan turning her in? Because you thought he was different, a small thought sparked within her mind that only made her even more furious.

It was clear to her now that she cared about Nathan, she probably would have loved him if everything had gone further. And with this realisation, only distress and regret greeted her. She was thoughtless and irrational despite her best efforts to be different with this man to how she was with her father or Shane. Kim felt much worse than shame then.

"You told me you wouldn't hurt her, you told me you wouldn't arrest her and that you just wanted to take her in for questioning. We made a deal after I first talked with you."

"I don't make serious deals with agents who don't follow instruction. This would never have happened if you had done what we asked of you in the first place." Nathan's boss brushed shoulders with him as he barged past, their conversation going unheard by Kim who was still shouting abuse from down the hallway.

And just like that, Nathan's hopes of being with Kim after all this situation settled down were crumbled. All he could hear were Kim's last words before they entered the elevator. They seemed to repeat over and over in his mind like a broken record even after the doors binged closed and she had disappeared.

"I hate you Nathan. I should never have trusted you. I hate you!"